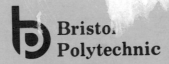

THE COAL HOUSE

THE COAL HOUSE

Andrew Taylor

COLLINS

William Collins Sons & Co Ltd
London · Glasgow · Sydney · Auckland
Toronto · Johannesburg

First published 1986
Second impression 1987
© Andrew Taylor 1986

British Library Cataloguing in Publication Data:
Taylor, Andrew
    The coal house.
    I. Title
    823'.914[F]   PR6070.A78

ISBN 0 00 184843-7 (hardback)
ISBN 0 00 184844-5 (paperback)

Typeset by Columns of Reading
Printed and bound in Great Britain
by Robert Hartnoll (1985) Ltd, Bodmin

For my family
and for everyone
in the smallest town I know

*The heart has its reasons which are
quite unknown to the head.* Pascal

Chapter 1

Alison lingered over packing her last case, as if she could postpone the moment of departure. She found herself remembering some of the conversations she'd had since sentence had been passed.

With her good friend Sal . . .

"What you going up *there* for?"

"Dad," Alison had said, ducking the question.

"But what's *he* going to do up *there?*"

She wished Sal wouldn't make the place sound worse than it almost certainly was.

"He's doing consultancy work for the University there. When he's not sitting at home writing his blessed textbooks. And he says it's honester up there. Cleaner. Says I'll like it. Says all sorts." A pause. "And anyway, since Mum."

Sal, who relished Sunday afternoon TV movies, said that you couldn't run away from memories.

"Better than sitting on top of them," Alison had snapped, surprised that, for the first time, she had made what amounted to a defence of Dad's decision to move North. Sal hadn't noticed.

"What about school?"

"Dad says there's a good comprehensive in the next village to ours. Says it's small, sort of an annexe to a bigger one, but dead good."

"They all say that." Sal mimicked, badly: " 'Our Sally's at a very good school, really excellent, reeeeally first class.'

They'd look prats if they said 'Sally's at a dumbo dump for cretins, the Headmaster smacks the sherry bottle every break, Mr Corder keeps looking at his watch as if he's timing a race, Mrs Carter and Frank Fitness are having it off and no-one knows how to work the computer.' "

They laughed. It was all true. The bell went for Maths.

Later, with her lovely, think-both-sides, nobody's-completely-wrong Gran . . .

"Ally, love, think how exciting it'll be! A new home, new friends, new places to see, a lovely garden, it'll be fun! Why, I bet Sal and the others would give their eye teeth to be going."

Would they hell, thought Alison.

Nevertheless, she loved listening to her Gran's enthusiasms, poured out in what was left of a lilting Irish accent. It didn't matter that Gran had got it wrong. The last thing Alison wanted was anything new. She wanted everything she'd known all her life. Familiarity. Certainty. Nothing new until she said so herself. Alison hadn't said as much to Gran: she loved her Gran and appreciated the careful thoughts.

She'd been living with Gran and Grandpa since the old house was sold and Dad had gone North to take a flat and house-hunt. One weekend there had been a letter for her from Dad, sounding too cheerful to be believable. There had been one for Gran in the same package. Alison noticed that both letters were separately sealed. Gran looked serious while she read hers, which was unusual: she was in the habit of reading out snippets and discussing them, taking half an hour to finish two sheets of tattle. Not this time.

Dad had found a house, Alison read in her own letter. But then he started using jargon. She'd noticed it before, among her friends' parents: when they were buying houses they were always talking about it and sounding as if they understood what was going on. Dad mentioned "an absentee vendor", said that he was due to "exchange

8

contracts" and that "completion can be expected within the month". Why couldn't he simply tell her when the Dreaded Day was going to come? Instead, he told her that he had sent down some colour photographs that the estate agent had given him. She noticed they'd come in Gran's envelope rather than her own and felt miffed. Gran finished her letter, put it away thoughtfully, looked at Alison for a moment and suddenly brightened up again.

"Come on," she said and spread the photographs out on the dining room table, shoving the tea things aside.

"Look, Ally, isn't it great?"

She had to admit, but didn't, that it was unlike anywhere she'd seen before.

It was a big, sprawling place, partly hidden by tall trees. In one of the photographs she saw a tall wooden verandah, with a balcony on the upper floor. It was painted white, but the paint was peeling.

"Like *Gone With The Wind*."

"Just what I was going to say, isn't it exactly the thing!"

There were photographs of the inside of the house. Tall ceilings, big windows, a posh staircase. There were pictures of the garden. It was very big and seemed completely overgrown, with trees all round it and, peeping up from the beanstalk weeds, a greenhouse you could park a bus in. On one of the outside pictures, Dad had put a cross on an upstairs window and written ALLY'S BEDROOM.

"Oh great, I don't get a choice, then!"

"Ah well, now, there may be all sorts of reasons, and anyway, I'm sure it's lovely. See, it'll look out over the garden, you'll have lots of fun taking your new friends up there."

"What new friends? Anyway, it isn't an attic room, I told Dad I wouldn't move unless I had an attic room with one of those funny windows."

She was behaving badly and she knew it, but Gran pretended to ignore the fact.

"Ah, that's all very fine and large, sweetie, but attic bedrooms don't grow on trees these days."

9

That conversation ended in giggles, too. Gran was nobody's fool.

And then there had been the conversation with her older cousin, Stuart, down from the Midlands for a weekend at Gran and Grandpa's.

Stuart was heavily into football, cars, bikes and equally predictable nonsense. At the same time, she liked him in a wary way. He played the piano much better than she ever could, even though he hated it as much as she. He was always kind to her. She found herself doing herself up a bit more than usual when she heard he was coming. After all, you could marry your cousin, couldn't you, and she had her future to think of. A few years time, and he might be the one to rescue her from the Dread North. She could always divorce him after, like Sal's Mum and Dad.

"Hey, it's a bit tasty," grunted Stuart, looking at the pictures. His voice had recently and finally broken, after years of swoops, squeaks and honks.

"It's all right, if you like that sort of thing."

"I wouldn't know, I've never had that sort of thing. Can't stand our new house. You can never get a place to yourself, always someone barging in on you. You should be all right in this place for that."

"Oh sure, stuck all alone, miles from anywhere, with just woods and weeds for company."

"You'll have the telly. And anyway, your Dad works at home now, doesn't he?"

"Sometimes," she said grudgingly, though she knew it was virtually true. "But I suppose he'll keep going off on trips or taking girlfriends for long weekends."

There had been a fragile pause. It was a day in March. Alison's mother had died the previous November. The last time she had seen her cousin was at the grey funeral, when he and the other members of her far-flung family had behaved towards her with hurtful distance. Gran had told her it was because they didn't know what to say, but

10

anything would have been better than silence and their tentative smiles. She had forced herself to stay aloof, keeping close to Gran, Grandpa and Dad. She had only cried later, in bed. Then, she had cried.

Stuart's curiosity about Alison's changing life suddenly got the better of him.

"What do you mean? Think your Dad'll get married again, or what?"

"If he does," said Alison airily, "I shall kill him."

That conversation did not end with laughter.

And now she was on the station platform in London, saying goodbye to Gran and Grandpa. Her cases were already stored in the Inter-City, her reserved seat had been located and Gran, with an out-of-date idea of how life was conducted on a busy, modern train, had asked the ticket inspector to "keep an eye on my grand-daughter. She's travelling alone, but she's being met." The inspector had looked nonplussed and said "Do what I can, darling". Alison had squirmed with embarrassment.

A stranger boarding the train would have seen an elderly couple, neatly dressed and clearly distressed at saying their goodbyes to a dearly-loved grandchild. But the stranger would not necessarily have seen a child. Alison, 13 years old, was tall for her age, as tall as Gran. She had long, very blonde hair, which she had put up, making her look even older. She wore a little make-up subtly applied. The padded ski jacket, blue sweater, tight jeans, dayglo socks and trainers tugged her apparent age down a little, but not a great deal. Alison Lucas was a handsome girl, with a knack of looking and sounding completely in control of herself and her surroundings.

Inside, she was wailing with apprehension. Not for the train journey, she had travelled alone before and enjoyed the grown-upness it made her feel. She was thinking of the journey's end.

Then, she was in her window seat, Gran and Grandpa

outside, waving and blowing kisses. It was that aching period before a train starts. On the table in front of her were a picnic box, a flask of pop, a bag of last-minute sweets bought by Grandpa, a copy of *Jane Eyre* and three girls' magazines. Alison was under no illusion that she would read them in that order. She would postpone the moment when she had to start improving herself, a phrase she noticed Dad was using more and more since Mum left.

There was a shiver, running through the train. Up front, the big diesel muttered to itself. Gran planted a kiss on the window, Grandpa smiled fiercely and waved frantically, Alison smiled and fluttered her fingers, not wanting to make too big a fuss in front of the other passengers.

Then, the train slid away. Gran and Grandpa started to trot along the platform to keep her in view as long as possible, but the train's acceleration soon beat them and they were gone. Alison had one squint back over her shoulder, but a trolley of mail bags had hidden them from her sight.

The train burst out into an April morning of washed blue and white sky, swung round a long curve and put its head down for the North.

Alison found a Kleenex and got rid of the one, shaming teardrop she hadn't quite been able to keep inside.

The rabbit came, cautiously, out of its burrow on the edge of the field and sat up, scenting the morning air. It sensed wetness, mist, a light, salty breeze, but no danger. Hopping down on to the field, it turned left and travelled ten metres, pausing twice to check the air. Then it jumped back up the small bank and lolloped into an old orchard, choked with nettles, thistles, willow herb, among which were ancient gooseberry bushes and stunted, barren apple trees.

The rabbit was hidden underneath the thick growth until it reached a gap in a hedgerow. Beyond lay a wide, shaggy lawn, untended for years. The lawn ran right up to a sprawling house with blind windows and a towering timber

12

verandah, its paint peeling. The rabbit took its bearings, carefully, sitting motionless for perhaps ten minutes. Somewhere in its body-memory stayed the experience of young, growing vegetables. It hopped out on to the lawn and skirted some tall sycamores, heading to the right of the house and towards the gardens.

Crouching low, behind one of the oak pillars of the old verandah, the fox watched. It lay as still as a bronze carving, its wise eyes apparently disinterested. It simply watched, and watched.

The rabbit, bolder now with the continuing lack of seen or scented danger, reached the edge of the old kitchen garden. Ahead was a forest of weeds and tall thistles. The rabbit's sense was correct: the previous spring they had been fewer and lower and had stood between the house and the vegetable plot, rich in food. The rabbit scented again, nose and whiskers tickling the wet air, but the light breeze was behind it and gave nothing away. It rose on its back legs once more, questing.

The fox exploded into movement.

The rabbit covered no more than a few metres before the fox brought it down. The woods winced with the high shriek of a death, a shriek which seemed to go on too long for an animal with a fox's teeth in its neck. Eventually, there was silence again, except for the slight whispering of sycamore leaves and the swish of grass as the fox trotted into the trees, carrying the rabbit in its mouth.

The rain came harder, dripping from the white verandah.

Chapter 2

Alec Lucas came out of the solicitor's office in the heart of the old city and stood for a moment, zipping his windcheater and pulling on his old tweed cap that had seemed affected in the South, but fitted his new surroundings. He savoured the cool air, the mist, the drizzle. It was a busy morning, traffic nudging over cobblestones, shoppers dawdling or scurrying. The cloud cover was so low it capped the cathedral tower. He could just see the cathedral clock: two hours until he met her train.

He thought: this morning the radio said it was fine and sunny in London. I wanted it to be like that for her when she got here. I wanted her to see everything looking its best. Just my rotten luck.

He thought again: but it's often like this up here. Perhaps it's better she sees it this way. When the sun comes, it'll be better for her.

Then he thought: oh hell, what does it matter either way?

He walked slowly towards the Market Place. The meeting at the solicitor's office had finished everything. The house was his. That bank on the corner of the Market Place now held what money he had. The removal van was somewhere on the motorway, carrying his furniture, his beds, books and carpets. Ally's train would be somewhere in the South Midlands. This was it. He lived here. He was scared.

He bought a newspaper, went into a pub, ordered a pint of beer and a packet of cheese and onion crisps, sat on a window seat and tried to read the news.

As always when he was alone and worried, he started a conversation with his dead wife.

"Do you think I should have stayed where I was?"

"You said you couldn't live there after I'd gone."

"But is it fair on Ally?"

"Children get over these moves much more quickly than we think."

"I'm not so sure about that."

"Well, neither am I really, but there's some truth in it. But look, I've only been gone a few months, love. She's still growing into that. That's a big change – the move is a smaller change."

"But it's me that's making it for her. She's got no choice in the matter."

"That's called being grown-up."

"I only liked the idea of being grown-up when I wasn't. Now I am, I don't think I am."

"Don't worry. It passes."

A party of suited men boiled into the pub, ordering beer and pasties. They were happy and loud. He watched them, remembering what it had been like to work for someone, to have an hour's lunch break, to make the same jokes to the same people every morning. At least all that was over.

They had interrupted his conversation with Helen, so he took a pen from his windcheater pocket and made a list of things to be done, using the margin of his newspaper.

> *2.15. Meet train.*
> *Take A. to house.*
> *3.00. Van due to arrive. (?)*
> *Make beds.*
> *Cook meal.*
> *Central heating (?)*
> *Light fire!*

It was confused, the sort of list that raised more problems than it solved.

Using the coin box in the pub, he called the local

Electricity Board. Yes, he had been connected and the meter had been read. He phoned the phone people. Yes, his line was operating and new directories were in the hall. He went to a supermarket and bought frozen peas, baked beans, sausages, tea, eggs, pies, fruit and Alison's favourite cereal. He knew he should buy more, or different, items, but he hated shopping. Helen would have done it better. But there.

He called at the Estate Agent's office and collected the keys to his house. They were ordinary keys, but they felt strange and heavy to his hand. He eventually rediscovered his car in a complicated multi-storey car park and edged it out into the city traffic, through the rain. It was now so gloomy that cars drove with sidelights or even headlamps lit, making yellow ripples on the wet roads. He drove up the hill to the railway station, parked the car, checked the timetable for the ninth or tenth time and sat on a bench on the platform.

After all that, he still had half an hour to spare.

The public address system in the carriage crackled, and a whiny voice warned her that the train was approaching the station and would she make sure she collected all her luggage, thank you. Well aware of where she was, or ought to be by now, she was already standing by the door, her cases at her feet, her shoulder bag stuffed with books, magazines, comics and the empty picnic box. She felt tired and slightly grubby with travel.

Two Japanese tourists were standing by the opposite window, peering out at the approaching city. They rattled excitedly and pointed. Trying not to appear curious, she peeked over their shoulders and saw the Cathedral and Castle, perched on their hill, solidly magnificent. The whole city looked cramped, buildings jumbled together round the feet of the two great constructions. It reminded her of a stylised drawing of a medieval town in one of her history books. A school book, no longer hers. It would be on the shelf in the Second year classroom, back home.

16

Stop it. Don't cry now.

The train slid to a halt and there he was, looking as untidy as ever. They got the cases out together, even though the Japanese tried to climb through first, then they hugged one another clumsily.

"Good trip?"

"Yeah, all right."

"Car's through here."

In the car park, she shivered. It was much colder than she'd been used to. The air smelled different. Wetter and cleaner. There was something else, a dusty, meaty smell, faint but unmistakable.

"Dad, what's that funny pong?"

"You know me, love, I couldn't smell a kipper under me conk." nose

"Sort of burny smell."

"Ah, that'll be the coal fires, I expect. Smoke."

As they drove through the city, he started to point places out to her.

"That's the Cathedral . . ."

"You don't say."

"Isn't it splendid?"

"A good Cathedral, not a great Cathedral."

"There's the river. There are lots of bridges. You can row on it."

"It's all water under the bridge."

"This is the road out. We live about five miles away."

"Not yet we don't."

"Oh Ally, come on."

"Well."

It was a few weeks since she'd seen her Dad. He looked tired and she could swear there was more grey in his beard. She knew he was thirty-nine, but she thought of him as agelessly older, stuck in a chunk of time that was occupied only by parents and teachers. She had to admit he looked better than Sal's Dad, or the fathers of most of her friends, who all wore suits and cardigans and naff track suits. He dressed in jeans or slacks, wore nice sweaters and bomber

17

jackets, had a beard, for heaven's sake, all his hair, most of his teeth and a pair of stylish, owlish spectacles. She didn't mind being seen around with him at all.

"Now then, watch, we're not far now."

He turned the car off a dual carriageway and they began to drop down a slope into a stretch of countryside. After the hustle of the rainy city, it was a motionless landscape. Ahead of her she saw a strange hill, an escarpment dotted with scrubby bushes. Below it lay a straggly village, half made up of pitmen's cottages, half of modern brick houses. In some trees stood a bleak church, and beside it what looked like an old and grand vicarage. There was a crowded graveyard.

The land seemed to billow, fields of cows curving suddenly and unexpectedly away to a gully where a pathetic stream struggled. Here and there were curiously regular humps, dotted with saplings and sparse grass, as if they were going bald.

"Those are the old pit heaps," said Dad. "They were levelled and grassed over during Reclamation."

"Levelled? You've got to be joking."

"Well, not levelled, brought down a bit. They used to be pretty high, apparently."

"Where were the coalmines, then?"

"Several pitheads. One over there. Another, I think, over there. I've got a map, we'll check."

"Doesn't matter."

"Then why did you ask?"

Alison shrugged and looked out of the window. They were coming down into the village now, the escarpment above them, the church hidden by trees and houses. The first thing she noticed was the contrast between the houses. Utilitarian rows of colliery boxes backed right on to the newer houses, which had bigger gardens and garages. Nevertheless, almost every house she saw was brightly painted, looked scrupulously clean. There were a great many cars, often rusty or patchworked with replaced body panels. There were no shops except a general Post Office and a butcher's.

18

Nothing was level, though nothing was steep. They swooped up, down and around the billowing landscape. The car left the village and climbed up a slope towards the summit of a hill. Alison saw a row of houses, falling away from the hilltop to her left. Dead centre was a big, stone-built public house. To her right was a ring of tall trees. It was towards the trees that Dad pointed.

"There you go. In there."

She sat still, unconcerned, but she was suddenly curious. In spite of the photographs, she did not know what to expect, but she knew that her first sight of her new home would be very important.

The car paused opposite the pub, turned sharp right and bounced down a driveway cratered with potholes, all filled with water. On either side were hedges of old, tangled hawthorn. Ahead were the trees.

"Gordon Bennett, you might have filled the holes in."

"They weren't mine to fill. Until today."

Through the ring of trees and into a gravelled turning circle. Dad stopped the car, put on the handbrake and switched off the engine. Silence, apart from the ticking of the cooling engine. She looked through the windscreen at the house.

It was big. Too big. How could she and Dad fill all those rooms? It was grey and wet. Looking at the photographs with Gran she had gained the impression of rosy coloured stone. She realised now that the cunning estate agent had photographed the house towards sunset on a fine day. The roofs were flat, greasy slate, the walls of grim stone blocks. The windows were black with emptiness. To one side lay a stable block, converted into two garages, but a stable block nonetheless: she saw the archway into what she supposed would be a stableyard if it hadn't been converted into a gin and tonic patio. In front of the house was a wide, semi-circular lawn, fringed by trees. Behind the house, she could only guess at the wilderness she had seen in the photographs. No sign of the verandah. It must be behind.

Now that the car was stopped and the windscreen wipers

19

still, the rain splintered her view of the house, breaking it up into a badly fitting mosaic.

"Well, what do you think?"

"I never know what to think when people ask me what I think."

"Let's go and see it."

They walked round the right side of the house, past some weatherbeaten outhouses, and came out upon the big back lawn. On her right, Alison saw the bank of trees running away down the side of the lawn before curving back and sealing off the entire property. To her left stood the white verandah. It looked impressive, but at the same time decayed, like the wedding cake of a jilted giant.

Dad put his arm across her shoulders, which was a good feeling. They walked through long, wet grass and stood in the shelter of the balcony. The big lawn was behind them now, ahead lay the jungle of weeds, the greenhouse roof surfacing briefly, the outline of the kitchen gardens glimpsed here and there and, of course, the continuous rain.

"Well," said Dad, "shall we go inside?"

"Might as well."

He fumbled through the keys on his ring and, on the second attempt, found the one which opened the french windows under the verandah. They stepped into a big room with parquet flooring, a marble fireplace and a high ceiling, decorated in the centre with an elaborate rose of plasterwork. There were tall casement windows on each side, bleeding grey light into the dusky space. There was no furniture. Dad switched on the bracketed wall lamps which ran right round the room and the weak bulbs filtered through faded red shades.

"Used to be a ballroom, apparently."

"Gordon Bennett."

"I do wish you'd stop saying that. I'd rather you swore, actually."

The air in the ballroom smelled still and stale. Her footsteps echoed loudly as she wandered round, seeing carved, built-in cupboards, an elaborate dado, rich wainscotting. At the far end of the room was a massive pitch pine panelled door with a brass handle. When she opened it, it swung heavily and smoothly away from her: its far side was covered in green baize. Beyond lay a dark corridor, leading to the house's main hallway and staircase, with one room off it, containing a trestle table and with an oddly incongruous modern glass-panelled door. It sat unhappily in the heavy house.

"Dad, can I go and wander about?"

"Of course. That's the idea."

He stayed in the ballroom, gazing at the empty fireplace and smoking a cigarette. He could hear his daughter's footsteps reverberating round the house, downstairs, then upstairs. He listened to her walk. Pause. Move. Walk again. He was picturing whereabouts she was at any moment, what she was seeing. Better for her to carry out the first exploration on her own.

There was a shrill squeal from upstairs. He walked briskly to the staircase and took the steps two at a time.

"Dad!"

"What is it?"

"We've got mice!"

He let the word 'we' live with him for a few seconds.

She was standing in the doorway of one of the empty bedrooms, not, thank heavens, hers. She wore a look of refined disgust and pointed towards a skirting board where a tell-tale gap led into darkness.

"There. It went in there. A mouse, or maybe a rat, even."

"We'll put down traps. We'll buy a cat. We'll call in the mouse people."

"Can we really buy a cat? Really?"

"Two. One to help the other. One for you, one for me."

"You won't forget, like usual? Promise."

"As good as done. So. What do you think of the place?"

She mooned round the room, looking at her feet, throwing a glance out of the window at the murky gardens.

"It's all right. For what it is."

"What is it?"

21

"A wreck. But it doesn't matter what I think, does it. I mean, you've bought it now. This is it. Finito."

Alison was using her nothing-to-do-with-me voice, flying her hands through the air. He looked at her, irritation rising. Surely she could make some effort to understand that this was their home now, that a smile and a deep breath would help things along. Her mother would have sailed into the situation, seeing only possibilities, not problems. He made an effort to stay calm, though he was saved by the sound of a truck blowing its horn somewhere at the front of the house.

What happened next lightened the glowering day. From the removal van climbed two stocky men in boilersuits, gazing pessimistically at the size of the house. They rolled fags and accepted tea from the electric kettle they took off the very back of the packed van. They were called Arnold and Vernon and had driven the long haul from the South in order to offload that afternoon. That way, they qualified for an overnight stop in a Northern hotel, with expenses and the prospect of a more leisurely drive home in the morning. Consequently, they put their backs into the unloading and worked until sweat sparkled in their hair, keeping up a constant banter along the lines that for one, Vernon, doors were always too narrow, stairs too steep, chairs too bulky, carpets too heavy while for Arnold all things were possible and why was he always saddled with a moaner and when Vernon had shifted as many loads as he, Arnold, had, he'd know a thing or two then.

In the middle of the afternoon there was another tea break, then they carried on. Alison kept out of the way, which was difficult. Whichever room she chose, Vernon or Arnold would immediately appear, straining and sweating, in the doorway with a grunted " 'Scuse me, darling, just got to roll this carpet down, could you, er . . ."

She left her Dad directing operations and wandered out into the garden where the mist still hung heavy under the trees and moisture soaked out of the still air. It would soon be prematurely dark.

A brick path led away from the house towards the kitchen

22

gardens, flanked on either side by the tall weeds which, she now saw, swarmed round some old gooseberry bushes, unpruned for years. At the end of the brick path was a square of short grass, kept down by use. It was overhung by a tall, leaning willow tree that looked good for climbing. The willow tree almost grew out of the brickwork base of the old greenhouse, which was long and wide, its back wall made up of part of the perimeter wall of the whole garden.

She pushed open a rickety wooden door and stepped inside the greenhouse. It was long and dim, the sloping glass roof stained and grimy above her. Weeds grew in the waist-high trenches of earth which were built of bricks dusty with a white deposit. In the back wall of the greenhouse were set square ventilation traps, worked by an iron lever: it was rusted stuck, the traps closed. Under the back trench was a cavern where, she guessed, heat would have fed into the greenhouse from a fire or a boiler. When she reached the far end she found a flat, brick working surface. It was piled high with old seed trays, pots, bottles and packets. None seem to have been used for years. As she moved her feet on the slatted floor, she heard dust whisper down into the heating cavern below, followed by a scurrying, scrabbling noise. More mice?

Very suddenly, she knew she was not alone. Now the mice were quiet, the greenhouse was silent, yet she felt eyes upon her. She turned slowly to face the still open door.

Outside, beneath the willow tree, stood a fox, one paw raised off the ground. It was motionless, gazing at her with incurious green eyes, its nose wrinkling at her. Girl and fox regarded one another like this for a long minute. Then Alison moved towards the door. The fox pricked its ears and let her reach the threshold of the door, a few metres away. Then it put its head down and trotted away down a garden path, purposeful but neither frightened nor panicked.

Alison followed, down through a tunnel of wet greenery. She came out in a vegetable plot, a surprisingly open stretch of bare earth, the size of a tennis court and surrounded by grass pathways. Here was the only sign of recent work in the

23

garden, for the soil had been neatly and thoroughly dug over. She could see no plants, though she noticed a worn garden spade standing in the earth at one end of the patch. And she saw the fox, on the far side of the turned earth, standing in a gap through a wall of overgrown raspberry canes, looking calmly back at her. As she watched, the fox turned once more and trotted through the gap into an area of long grass and gnarled old fruit trees.

"Do you want me to follow?"

When she reached the gap, there was no fox, but she could see a track through the wet grass, heading even further away from the house towards the high, far wall of the garden. She followed the track, which became darker and gloomier as it led under the trees. Her feet were soaking, her jeans damp and clingy to above her knees. The track simply petered out when it reached the wall, where she saw that some of the big, irregular quarry stones had fallen away, leaving a gap near the ground, a metre across. Through the hole, she saw the wood.

At this point, the sycamores formed more than a circle round the house and garden, they were a deep group of dark sentinels. Old, fallen trees zig-zagged beneath them in the undergrowth where the fox's regular trips had created a complete tunnel that disappeared into the wood. Rain dripped from the trees, a continuous rustle of water.

Crouching by the hole in the wall, she thought what good times she and Sal and the others could have had in the woods. Or she and Mum. The tears shone on her cheeks.

Standing and turning, she saw the house, all its lights on inside, blazing like a beached liner across the straggly garden and through the dripping trees.

Well, it was home. She'd just have to do something about it.

She walked back towards the house, wiping her eyes on her sleeve.

Much later that night, Alec Lucas stood on the balcony, looking away down over the gentle hills towards the city, where street lights scattered like distant sparklers. He was bone weary and in need of a bath he knew he hadn't the energy to take tonight. He sipped at a large whisky and let the night air dry his brow.

The carpets were down as much as they could be. The furniture was all in, even if not where it should be, although he remembered a saying of his own father's, "Where things go on moving-in day, that's where they'll stay." He had very probably been right.

He and Alison had taken Vernon and Arnold down the drive to the pub at about seven. There, they had eaten beefburgers, chips and peas, served with bread and butter and plastic containers of sauce labelled RED and BROWN. The removal men, belching, had wished them well and headed for their digs in the city.

Now, Alison was asleep. It was nearly midnight. They were both exhausted and she had fallen into bed willingly. He had a feeling that she had changed since the arrival and was, at least, allowing the new home to become more approachable. Maybe not.

He talked with his wife, a conversation held through the black night, the rain and the whisky glass.

"Well, we're in."

"What's it like?"

"Tatty. You'd love it."

"Ally?"

"Don't know. Very uppity at first. Nothing right. But she's, I'm not sure, accepting more tonight."

"Take care of her for me. I know she's young, but she's very womanly. We need looking after. Sometimes."

Silence. A sip.

Below him, in the woods, something crashed briefly and was still. He must remember about the cats.

"Are you still there, love?"

"Go to bed now. Sleep. Forget about everything until tomorrow."

"O.K."
And he did.

Chapter 3

Alison woke suddenly, in a panic. For several seconds she couldn't think where she was. When she remembered, she plumped her pillows, lay back and looked around her.

The bedroom was big and boxy, inelegantly shaped. Along one wall were flush, fitted cupboards, shelves and wardrobes. Their doors were snugly shut, made of solid timber. Her bed looked out of place: the same, familiar bumps and hollows, the duvet Mum had bought two birthdays ago, the same linen and pillow cases, but all in this strange, faraway room. Her dressing table had been piled high the previous night with bags of her books, games, treasures and a roll of her favourite posters. Two suitcases were still to be unpacked. On her bedside table stood a plate with an apple core and a mug of cocoa dregs. The wallpaper, slightly faded (she could see where pictures had once hung), was a pretty blue and white, matched by curtains. Dad had bought the curtains with the house. But he hadn't bought the sunlight which poured through them, making the room bright and cheerful.

"Take it easy, lady, don't rush anything."

Slowly, she swung her legs out of bed and turned to the window. Slowly, she opened the curtains and looked out.

She had never seen such blues and greens. The sky was a ceiling of eggshells, with a bright sun just clearing the furthest sycamores. Its light shattered off the greenhouse roof. The gardens were a jigsaw of dark, medium and light

27

greens, with hints of the pathways snaking to and fro. The courtyard was still mottled by the night's heavy rain, but steaming and drying fast. Spring birdsong filled the air and she watched as bluetits, sparrows and two robins fluttered round an empty bird table, looking for scraps.

"That's something I can do, anyway."

Through the trees, black and white cows grazed on a gentle slope. She had never seen a garden so peaceful or full of life. It was wild, still wet, bursting at the edges and it was a million miles distant from the garden through which she had followed the fox. Over the wall, the shadows under the trees, already blue, enticed her.

Downstairs, a radio came on, playing heart-starting music. The kitchen clattered. She got out of bed completely, didn't wash, but dressed, rummaging a dry pair of jeans from one of her cases. She ran down the corridor and down the staircase, through the hall, the drawing room, dining room and into the kitchen. Dad was busy fiddling with the cooker.

"Blimey, you're dressed!" she said, with mock astonishment.

"Don't be cheeky. Country living. Early starts. Morning."

"Hi! What's for breakfast?"

"Eggs on toast."

"Yuk. Hey, what happened to the weather?"

"I changed it. It was a day late. Mind you, it always rains on moving-in days."

"I wouldn't know, I've never moved-in before."

"You moved into the world, babe. It was raining then, too, now I think of it."

Dad was, she thought, absurdly pleased about the fact that both milk and newspapers had been delivered on the very first day. She saw nothing magical about this, since it was the purpose of milk and newspapers and letters to be delivered. But whether because of this or for other reasons, Dad was definitely in a good mood and she decided that as long as he stayed that way, she'd make an effort to stay with him.

28

After breakfast, he dumped everything in the sink and took her upstairs to the balcony, where the sun had yet to reach and the morning air was still cold-water cool.

"Look. The Cathedral. Five miles away, that is."

It looked like an ordinary parish church, a stump of darker colour pointing upwards out of a layer-cake of greens and browns. On the furthest horizon, she saw high moors, dwarfing the city and its stump. Immediately below was more interesting. Criss-crossing the main lawn were animal tracks, bruised out of the dew-pearled grasses. They were of different sizes and patterns, zooming away in different directions.

"Dad, you know there's a fox? I saw it last night."

"Rabbits, too, I reckon. Moles, Hedgepiggies. 'The Questing Beast'. You name it."

"Shush."

"Come on, then."

"Where?"

"Bank. Shopping."

"Oh no, stroll on."

"For cats."

Billy the milkman parked his van behind the pub and began to heft a crate of bottles out of the back just as Harry the landlord opened the back door, wearing a dressing gown and slippers.

"Nice morning."

"Aye, cannier than I thought it would be, mind."

The pub was the last call on Billy's round and Harry always gave him a mug of sweet tea. They stood by the back door, considering the morning and watching the early city bus pause at the village stop to pick up no-one, drop off no-one, before grinding away down the lane.

"See they're in at the Coal House?"

"Aye. Came in here last night with his removal men, for a spot of supper, like. Can't stand moving houses, meself. Never could."

"Didn't see anyone. What are they like?"

"Hard to say," said Harry, lighting his first cheroot of the long, publican's day. "Him, he's about forty, well-spoken, bit scruffy, but that could just be moving day, couldn't it. Got a beard, glasses. Nice daughter, big girl, don't know, mebbes fourteen or so. Blonde girl, very quiet. No wife, like."

"She'll be coming later on, I suppose."

"I've got a feeling. Divorced, or widowed, mebbes. Just a feeling it's just them two."

"In the Coal House? Why, they'll rattle like beans in a balloon."

"No accounting."

"I remember when the colliery managers lived there, you know, aye, and the old pit-owners before them. Why, there was always something going on there, man. Parties, meetings, dances. Garden fetes in the summer. They had three gardeners over there, two living in, and no end of servants. Wally's old Mam used to skivvy over there, after the First War. Bit different now. What's this new chap do, then?"

"Don't rightly know. Think he does something at the University, mebbes, but not full time, like."

"Think they'll settle?"

"If we let 'em."

"Aye. Thanks for the tea."

"You're welcome, William."

The Coal House had a history that stretched back into a storm of gritty dust, a clatter of pit wheels, a rattle of railway trucks, into deaths and births and rivalries that had soaked into its very stones.

It was a history in which Alison and her Dad were to provide, unexpectedly, an important link.

At the very start of the nineteenth century the village was tiny, a collection of farmworkers' cottages set at the joining of the boundaries of three handsome farms. The villagers

30

drew their water from a pump, stabled their horses in an old barn and worked the land all around. Elsewhere, the Industrial Revolution was in full, smoky gallop, crying out for coal to keep alive. Coal was black gold.

One day, towards the harvest of 1819, a mining engineer visited one of the farmers. He stayed a few days and when he left, suddenly the rumour was out and running through the village. Coal had been discovered under the farmland, a rich, deep seam. The farmer, a quiet man and a Justice of the Peace, was in torment. He loved his land and he loved farming. If he mined it, he knew he would become ten times wealthier almost immediately. He also knew that the earth would be ripped apart, the land raped. He knew that men, women and children would be gulped into the ground, coal would be vomited back, spoil heaps would blacken the sky and machinery would shriek in the night. For that autumn and through to the next spring, he continued to farm his acres.

The other two farmers had no such compunction. When the seam was found to cross their farms, they began to mine. The earth was opened. Desolation began. The farmworkers exchanged the vagaries of the weather and the wilfulness of the crops for the filth and dangers of life underground and a steady wage.

The Justice of the Peace turned his face to the wall and died of a broken heart as his workers left him and poured into the mines. His son promptly began to mine the farm and the whole area was given over to coal. Terraces of grubby houses crawled outwards, transforming the village. One farmer, richer than the others because his coal was superior, bought them out and began to consider himself the new Lord of the Manor, the Industrial Aristocrat.

He built himself a house that would tell the world how lofty he had become. He was a small-minded man, greedy for recognition. Plans were changed, sudden whims incorporated, architects dismissed. The house grew unevenly, sprawling with last-minute thoughts and improvisations.

One architect brought a little grace to it: the well-proportioned frontage that overlooked the great lawn, the hand-carved pitch-pine verandah and balcony, and, at the pit-owner's order, high stone walls round the gardens and a circle of sycamore trees to screen off the sight of the growing coal tip and sprouting winding gear. No sooner had the man arranged the Coal House, as the villagers dubbed it, than he died and a new owner moved in to start alterations.

Owners came and went.

One family in particular had an influence on the area that was to echo down the years and touch Alison and her Dad. But the family's circumstances were complex, little understood and shadowed with sadness: the village, by and large, soon forgot them. Only one man carried their story forward into the future.

That future brought nationalisation of the coalfields. Now, the Coal Board put its pit managers into the Coal House as one of the perks of the job. The old house, denied its armies of servants, began to suffer. The gardens grew slowly ranker.

About the time men first walked on the moon, the coal all but ran out. It became too expensive to mine. The pits were closed and capped off. Rows of miners' cottages were pulled down, railways ripped up. The Miners' Institute, chapel and school disappeared. The population sank from over two thousand to less than two hundred. Those that remained took retirement or travelled to nearby pits that still worked. They all watched with wry smiles as the great irony took form: the scarred, heaped moonscape melted away, the land was lowered and returned to fields, ramblers and horse-riders from the city appeared. Wheat, potatoes and rape grew on the once raped, strangely curving countryside. Just occasionally, a man digging his allotment would turn up a nugget of shiny black and know, by its feel, where it had come from. Just occasionally, a crack would snake along someone's bedroom wall as the land settled gently over its warren of empty passages and caverns.

A succession of distant people lived at the Coal House,

32

shutting themselves away from the village. The driveway became pocked with craters. The paint peeled on the verandah. In the garden, a few flowers struggled against the weeds and gave up. The roses went wild, the fruit bushes lank. Finally, one owner packed up and left for America. Men no longer walked on the moon. The village waited to see who they would get next at what some of them had taken to calling the Bad House.

They got Alison and her Dad who, in their turn, got a great deal more than they expected.

They were seven weeks old, tortoiseshell kittens with boot button eyes and tiny, pink noses. They were sisters, not highly bred but pretty and compact. That second evening, they lay in the same cot, made from a tomato tray and padded with old pullovers. There were two cots, but the young animals, agog with their new home, curled together for reassurance, their tummies full, their minds awhirl with new experiences, their instinct to sleep finally victorious.

"They'll have to sleep out when they're older," said Dad, because he thought he should.

"When they're older. When they've had their jabs. I've put a tray of cat litter by the kitchen door."

"We'll have to get them spayed. Not having the place crawling with moggies just because the local toms get into the garden."

Alison tickled the orange, black and startlingly white bundles. She called them Cubby and Maxi. For one of those reasons that has nothing to do with reason, Cubby was always Cubby and Maxi became Max.

That night, she woke in the small, dead hours, still with the feeling of surprise at her surroundings. Outside, a full moon painted the world with milk. She went downstairs, quietly, trying not to wake Dad in his balcony-bedroom. Cubby and Max were lying in a snoozing knot, their white tummies turned trustingly upwards.

At least she had some friends in the place now.

33

Dad, however, was awake and listening. He gazed at the ceiling, wondering if fluffy kittens were the right company for his daughter, whether they would tug her back into childhood instead of helping her forward into the business of growing-up. He asked his wife.

"We all," she told him, "need something to cuddle and call our own."

Chapter 4

It all began to happen on the first Saturday morning, when Alison found Tommy Saddler in the woods.

In the fourteen years that Tommy Saddler had been alive, he had collected three brothers, two sisters, a terrier and an air rifle. Of these, the terrier and the rifle gave him the most fulfilment. Tommy, after all, was an expert rabbiter. He was so good that harassed gardeners and allotment owners and even farmers paid him to keep the rabbit population down to manageable levels. Sometimes they paid him and let him keep the rabbits for the Saddler kitchen; sometimes they bought the rabbits for their own pots. Either way, Tommy was provided with a small, welcome income. He needed it. His Dad, who worked at the mine a few miles away, was on strike with the rest of them and pocket money had dried up weeks before. No miner's family had spare cash. They had already sold what they could. Tommy's Dad was the only miner to have kept his car, which all the families helped to tax and run, sharing it when they needed to travel. TV sets had been returned to the rental companies. Holidays had been cancelled. Shoes were repaired and pullovers patched.

Tommy was finding the cost of airgun pellets a strain.

He favoured an expensive brand, two pounds fifty for five hundred, but he considered them worth it. He could knock over a bunny at several hundred metres range and rely on the terrier to finish it off and retrieve. His rifle was a maximum velocity .22 German weapon. It had come to his wondering hands one birthday, when his Dad won first prize in the local Leek Show. His Dad had not only tabled the winning pair of prize leeks, his Dad had broken records. He had taken first prize for his tray of mixed vegetables, for his dressed onions, for his chrysanthemums and for his buttonhole. The accumulated prize money was considerable. The whole Saddler family benefited but Tommy, whose birthday fell a week after the Leek Show, benefited more than most. Within a year, his was the name mentioned when rabbits savaged young plants or burrowed and bred by the beet fields.

Tommy had no commission that Saturday morning. For his own pleasure he whistled up the terrier and left the village, passing the pub and heading down the bank beside the Coal House woods. At the back end of the woods was an overgrown, broken gate. He ducked under and walked softly into the trees. The terrier, used to these trips, quivered around Tommy's feet, resisting the urge to rush ahead. Boy and dog followed the route of the old carriage drive, which curved through the wood, heading for the Coal House, which he could just make out through the trees, its white verandah gleaming in the morning light. He had known the Coal House grounds all his life and had been chased out of the woods countless times. But Tommy had been spending a few half term days with his aunt on the coast and, as far as he knew, the Coal House was still standing empty.

He approached the point where the old drive left the trees and headed out over the main lawn. He paused, crouched and patted the dog down into the grass. There were four or five rabbits on the far side of the lawn, hopping and halting their cautious way up the side of the hedgerow, looking for food. Tommy pumped his rifle, slipped a pellet into the barrel, closed it up and sighted carefully. The terrier nearly exploded with anticipation. There was a crack, a brown and white shape jumped and fell, the other rabbits fled in all directions and the terrier streaked across the lawn.

"Hey. What are you doing?"

36

It was Tommy's turn to jump. She came through the trees behind him, from the direction of the Coal House, a tall, blonde girl about his age, wearing blue denim dungarees. He'd been caught. At least it wasn't a grown-up. She talked with an accent that was very hard to follow.

"Rabbits."

"But. This is our garden, sort of."

"Pardon me?"

"You can't just come wandering in with a gun. How would you like it?"

"Aye, well, no rabbits in our garden, like, so it'd be a waste of time, wouldn't it."

There was a squeal of death from the far side of the lawn. He'd got one, at least. Perhaps if he offered it to the girl she'd keep quiet?

"There are kittens round here, you see. You could kill one of them."

"Don't shoot cats. Can't eat 'em."

"Well I don't eat rabbits."

Bugger, that was a good idea down the drain.

"What about your Mam and Dad. Would they like a bunny for the pot, like? Can have it if you want."

"There's only me and Dad. Mum's dead."

"Live in the Coal House, do you?"

"Moved in Thursday."

"Where you going to school?"

"Pitclose Village Comp. Start next week."

"I go there."

Keep her talking, he'd get out of this yet.

"I'd have thought you was too posh for our school. Big house, like."

"I'm not posh."

Tommy risked standing up and looked sceptically up the lawn to the white verandah, the sprawling stonework.

"Just two of you. In that."

"We lived down south. Houses cost a lost more there. When we sold ours, Dad could afford to buy something bigger up here. That's all."

37

"All that for two people."

"It's an investment. We haven't got anything else."

Tommy was going to remark that some people round here didn't have anything, full stop, when the terrier swished back through the grass, awkwardly tugging the dead rabbit by its broken neck. Tommy noticed with disgust that it was a young doe without much meat. Alison regarded it with curiosity.

"You really going to eat that?"

"Why aye, why not? Not very big, like, but it'll do for the pot."

"What do you do with the skins?"

"Hoy 'em away, they're nae use, man."

"You could stitch them all together, make a cloak. Or a coat or a hat or somesuch."

Bugger, she was a weird one, this. She wouldn't last long in 2A.

Back in the house, Dad was having his own meeting.

He had been sitting on a stool by the window, sipping tea and reading the newspaper: the pros and cons of the miners' strike took up two whole pages. Now he lived in a coalfield, he felt he should follow the dispute more closely, though it was really an excuse to put off doing any work.

Suddenly, the electric kettle began to boil. He put down the paper and looked at it. It was over two metres away from him, on the opposite work surface, plugged in but not switched on. It had simply decided to boil up on its own.

"Well I'm damned."

"Aye, you'll find that up here."

Dad started. Standing in the open door was a solid man in a blue boiler suit and a woolly bobble cap. He was smoking a curly pipe and holding a ball of orange bailer twine in oil-blackened, stubby fingers. He had silvery hair and a wind-tanned face.

"It's the electrics, you see. Very poor supply round here, you see, like the water. We get our electrics from the sub

38

generator over by Cleedon Gate. Surges a lot. Cuts out pretty often, and all. You get a surge, it often trips a switch, like. You get kettles boiling, lights flickering. Once it switched on a ring on the wife's cooker."

"Thank God for that. I thought we had ghosts."

The man looked cryptic: "You might at that, mind. There's been enough funny things happened here . . ."

"Yes. Can I help you at all?"

"Well, you see, I come with the house, in a manner of speaking. If you want me, like, or tell me to bugger off if you wish, no offence taken."

Dad had a suspicion what was coming and he was right.

"I do the garden for whoever's living here, you see. Well, not everyone who's lived here, but some of them have used me. Not the last lot, but I came in anyway and kept the vegetable plot turned over and fed."

"I saw that. It looks good soil."

"Oh, it's canny soil all right, no mistake. It's been well fed through the years and all. Farmyard muck, fertiliser from the farm. I work on the farms, you see, round and about. I used to come here for a few hours at the weekends, set the plants away, tidy up. You could feed yourselves from this garden, you know. Tatties, cabbages, leeks, lettuces, beans if you like them, grow anything if you've a mind to here, you know."

"I'm not much of a gardener. Never had much of a garden. Till now. My name's Alec Lucas."

"Peter Robson. Pleased to meet you, Mister Lucas."

God, his hands were like rough iron. He was a pleasant man, probably in his fifties, definitely local, the original horny handed son of the soil. Should he use him? He could do with the help.

"Cup of tea, Peter? Since the kettle's boiled for us."

"Aye, thanks very much. Two pound an hour."

"Ah, I was wondering."

He busied himself with the teapot. He had no idea whether that was a fair rate or not. He supposed he'd just have to calculate whether it was worth it to him to have help

39

with the vast, shaggy garden. He fancied the idea of home grown food, but had no notion of how to go about it. She would have known. She would have had a row of spuds in already. He handed Peter a mug of tea and made his mind up.

"All right, then, Peter. How about a fiver's worth a weekend."

"Two and a half hours, like. Aye, that'll make a start, at least."

Dad smiled ruefully. "I'm not very well off. Not as well off as some people who've lived here, I expect. That's all I could run to. For now, anyway."

"No, no, no, that's all right, that suits fine." Peter Robson looked embarrassed. They never discussed money again. Dad would hand Peter a fiver and, quite often, more: Peter would slip it into his wallet without a word. Eventually, as the summer grew, they would walk across to the pub after working in the garden. Dad would buy Peter a pint, then Peter would break into the fiver to buy Dad a pint in return. Alison called it daft, "The Peter Routine", but its easy familiarity pleased Dad enormously. And, through Peter, Dad became hooked on gardening.

They sipped their tea, sitting on kitchen stools in the sunlight and finding out about one another. Peter was the son of a tenant farmer. They had worked a prize farm some miles away, owned by the local brewery. It was to have been Peter's, but the brewery would not renew the tenancy and took the farm back.

"Buggers, they were. Killed me Dad."

Now Peter lived in the next village and freelanced for the local farmers.

"Combining. Tractor work. Bit of everything, like. That's another thing. I can get you good plants and seed, spot of fertiliser, better than you'd get in the shops, mind."

"Don't the farmers mind?"

"Why no, man, not if it's me. Did you have any ideas about that old greenhouse?"

Dad hadn't, but it quickly became clear that Peter Robson

had. They would grow tomatoes and bring on the young plants, 'set them away'. So that was all right. Dad wondered if Peter's meter was already ticking.

There was a movement, out beyond the courtyard. Cubby and Maxi came racing, pell mell, out of the undergrowth, across the yard and through the kitchen door, their tiny claws skidding on the floor tiles as they bolted into the depths of the house. Following behind them, stepping into the courtyard came Alison and a boy carrying a rifle and a rabbit. There was a terrier, which would have been the one to put the frights up the kittens, who had never seen anything else on four legs except their mother and litter mates. So who was the boy? Peter Robson obviously knew. He muttered "Yer bugger!" and stepped out into the yard, hands on hips. The boy faltered.

"Tommy Saddler, yer little bugger, ye've been shooting in Mister Lucas's garden, get away with you, lad, go on."

"Might have known you'd soon get your feet under the table, man," said Tommy, scornfully and Dad thought sadly how little he knew about local relationships, how much he'd have to learn.

"Well, wait a minute," he said, but Peter was in charge now.

"Why no, man, give this one an inch, he'll be all over the place, lifting your vegetables, pinching your fruit, you'd have no peace. Away!"

"He shot a rabbit," said Alison, unnecessarily.

Tommy had a last attempt, holding the dangling doe towards Dad.

"Aye. Do you want it, Mister? For the pot? It's not very big, like, but it'll cook well enough."

"Um. I'm not very good with rabbits, I'm afraid."

"Can we keep it, Dad? I want to make something with the skin."

"Oh yes? And who's skinning it, then?"

"Why, if you really want it, I'll do that for you," said Peter, hedging his bets as to who was in the ascendancy.

"Well. All right then. Thanks, er, Tommy is it?"

Tommy pressed home.

"You've got a lot of bunnies down by," he said, tossing his head backwards. "They'll get your plants, like. I could knock a few off for you, if you like."

"You little bugger," said Peter. Dad looked from one to the other, then at Alison, mutely asking for feminine advice.

"What I thought, Dad, was that if we got more, I'd stitch the furs together to make a cloak. And it would save your plants, wouldn't it?"

"What bloody plants? Haven't put any in, yet."

This, Dad saw, was a morning for instant decisions.

"OK, Tommy, but listen. If you want to shoot rabbits, you can. But just you, nobody else, right? And you knock on the front door first and ask me, right? There may be times when I don't want a lethal marksman stalking through the woods. And those kittens are still pretty young, they haven't been inoculated yet, so keep your dog away from them, please."

He took the rabbit from Tommy's hand. Tommy glanced at Peter, triumphantly. He'd listened hard to the man's funny accent and he had a fair suspicion he'd won the round.

"Aye, OK Mister. Thanks very much like. I'll do you a good job, mind. Tommy Saddler's the best bloody rabbiter for miles."

Dad, amused, turned to Peter Robson, who was sulking. "Well, Peter? Is he?"

"He's not bad, like. But he's a little waster."

Peter took the rabbit from Dad's hand and produced a very big, very sharp clasp knife from one of his many pockets. Alison went hurriedly inside the house. Tommy gave a self-conscious wave and headed for home, whistling up the terrier. Dad and Peter regarded the dangling rabbit.

"Mister Lucas," said Peter thoughtfully, "tell me to mind me own business, like, but is it your opinion the lassie's serious about making something to wear with rabbit skins?"

"Can't tell with my daughter, Peter. Sometimes she gets an idea and sticks with it, sometimes she forgets about it in minutes. This sounds like a sticking idea, I think."

42

"Only y'cannot just use the skins like that, you know. They go stiff as plywood and pong. They need to be cured and that means acid baths and all sorts. Bit dangerous for a young lass, mebbes?"

"Ah. That's that, then."

Peter looked cunning and wise.

"Ah, wait a bit. My sister-in-law works at the Craft Centre on the new bridge in the city. Now they cure skins there, I know for a fact, they run these classes and that. If your lass gets the skins ready, washed, I'll see if my sister-in-law'll take 'em in once a week to be seen to."

"More expense," gloomed Dad.

"Why there are ways, man. Leave it with me." And Peter crouched down over the rabbit. The clasp knife flashed. Dad swallowed hard and went for a walk round the garden.

Following an afternoon with his wife's old cookbooks, Dad served jugged rabbit for supper. He surprised himself by enjoying it. Alison toyed with it, bravely. Dad explained about the complexities of having the skins cured, hoping it would put her off the whole idea. On the contrary, she took Peter's offer as confirmation that the project was possible and desirable.

As they washed the dishes after the first rabbit supper, Alison said, unexpectedly,

"Do you realise that since we've been here you haven't done a stroke of work?"

"No. I suppose not, really."

"Tomorrow's Sunday. You work. I'll do the other things. Cook, and, and, clean and stuff like that."

"Oh yes?"

"Yes!"

Dad was strangely happy. Alison was coming home.

Sunday was only a few minutes old when a light fret blew in from the coast and drifted through the Coal House woods, like strips of grey muslin against dark, dripping night. Under the wet leaves on the ground, small animals scurried, about their business.

In one of the tallest sycamores, the owl watched his world. He was in charge of the night. His round head swivelled, his eyes were caverns of seeing. He was tracing this mouse, that vole, the fat shrew, as they busied themselves below him. He was selecting his most likely victim.

He made his decision, spread his tawny wings and shuffled to the edge of his bough.

A twig snapped. Animals ran. The owl shrank back, head whipping round and down.

Steadily, through the wet woods, walked a tall figure in a black cloak and a wide brimmed black hat. It came from the old gate on the bank, retracing Tommy's steps of the morning. It strode onwards, without looking to left or right, familiar with the path through the hollies and elders. It reached the edge of the lawn, paused, then stepped out from the trees. It stood still and tall, a black pillar. It looked over to the scene of the rabbit's death, tracing the trail of bent grass where the terrier had sprinted and retrieved. Then it looked up at the Coal House, silent and dark except where the verandah glimmered.

The owl watched. The figure crouched, fingering the damp earth, then straightened and watched the house again. The owl stirred.

The figure turned and looked back, up into the sycamores. For a long moment, the two night creatures stared at one another, as if challenging for possession of the woods.

Then the owl spread its wings, sailed out and away, searching for other hunting grounds.

The black figure watched it go, then stalked slowly across the lawn and out through the hedgerow on the far side.

Under the trees, nothing living moved.

Chapter 5

On the first day of school after half term, Tommy Saddler woke with the dawn, as usual. He lay for a few minutes, listening to one of his brothers snuffling. In the room next door, his father was coughing, the deep, rattling coughs of the pitman and cigarette smoker. Tommy's bedroom smelled stale with sleep.

He got up quietly, scooped up his clothes from the end of the bed and took them to the bathroom. When he was dressed, he went down to the kitchen, heated up what was left of a can of baked beans, heaped them on bread and wolfed them down. He drank a pint of water, shrugged on his anorak, checked the pocket for airgun pellets, collected his rifle from its hiding place in the garden shed and set off down the street through the village.

He didn't pay much attention to the morning, which was perfect. The sky was pale blue, almost green in places, studded with small pink clouds which were catching the rising sun. The air was as cold as mountain water. In the woods beyond the cottages, the dawn chorus had started. Pit villages rise early and in several of the cottages lights were on and kettles boiling: the striking miners were lying awake in bed, but their wives, unable to break the habit, were up and doing. From most of the chimneys rose columns of still, yellow-grey coal smoke.

Tommy passed the pub and broke into open ground. He halted, scenting the air like an animal, then headed away to his right, to the village end of the Coal House driveway. He could just see the house through its barricade of trees, dark and quiet in the early morning.

From the end of the driveway, a public footpath struck away down the slope of the fields towards the next village. As Tommy padded down the path, the whole county opened before him. The curving fields and humping scarps cluttered away towards the distant city, where the stump of the cathedral tower rose above a drift of chimney smoke and the occasional early car semaphored the sunlight. Tommy kept his head down, watching for droppings and testing with a wet finger that the slight breeze was still blowing towards him. A hundred miles above him, a jet ruled a pink line across the sky.

At the bottom of the first field Tommy climbed over a stile and slowed as he edged beside a hawthorn hedge. He paused, crouched, peered, crawled a few yards and paused again. Through the hedge he could see a strip of allotments that filled in the land between the farmer's fields and the road. The allotments were spiked with scarecrows, criss-crossed with strings from which danced milk bottle tops, dotted with stakes from which flapped empty plastic bags. None of these devices deterred the rabbits that were worrying away among the carrot tops and young lettuces.

Tommy dropped his expected rabbit with his first pellet, but then he had a piece of luck. When the other rabbits bolted for safety, one, a big doe, became caught up in some netting that an allotment gardener had spread over his young plants. The doe struggled and twisted long enough for Tommy to reload and take leisurely aim. He didn't have the terrier with him, so in this case he had to squeeze through the hedge and finish the wounded doe by breaking her neck. The other rabbit was dead. Two kills. Two pellets. Tommy was impressed by himself.

He carried the rabbits back up the footpath until he reached the boundary of the Coal House land. He turned right and skirted it until he reached the woods. He ducked under the fence and into the trees until he reached the spot where the girl had disturbed him. Kneeling, he took out his knife, opened it and went to work.

Half an hour later, when Alison opened her bedroom curtains to the sun, she saw two smoke-grey rabbit skins, cleaned and neatly pegged to the clothes line.

Even later that morning, she saw something else: that schools, however different in style, however far apart, share many similarities.

She stood on the edge of the playground, waiting for the morning bell, her school case heavy. The morning playground was like any other. Groups of girls huddled together, whispering and sniggering. Rival groups batted sarcasm backwards and forwards. Chains of boys ran and whooped and punched and kicked a flaccid yellow and black football.

She thought of her school down South. She and Sal and the others would be huddled in just such a comforting group, probably throwing mild insults at Doreen Banks and her gang. Here, she had no group to join and was aware of a pricking behind her eyelids, a hardness in her throat, a shortness of breath.

Dad had dropped her off but had not come in with her. She wasn't sure whether she was glad or sorry.

The school didn't look at all like her last one, which had been a series of pavilions of steel and glass, set in acres of playing fields, bulging with equipment, blessed with an orange running track, crammed with computers, boastful of a full sized theatre with a microchip lighting console. Her new school was made of old, red brick. It had a bell tower and tall casement windows. The playground was a slab of tarmac the size of a football pitch. The playing field was a square of grass, scrubby with shrubs. The classrooms had old fashioned desks and wooden blackboards. On her introductory visit with Dad, she had met the headmaster, a pleasant, moley man, and her class teacher, Mrs Mallon, who was tubby, firm and friendly. The staff were all right. But that wasn't much help. Not now, as she stood in a

47

leper's solitude.

One of the groups of girls looked over towards her, whispered among themselves and burst into shrieks of cruel laughter, folding inwards upon themselves. Her tears were nearer.

"Come on, lovey, this won't do. This is the worst part. It'll get better once you're inside and the day's begun. Be brave."

"Oh Mum!"

The tears were solid in her throat now. She couldn't find a tissue in her anorak.

"Hey, this won't do. Where's my Ally? Come on, don't let Dad down. He loves you a lot, you know."

"He's got a funny way of showing it, dumping me down in this awful place. Oh Mum, why did you die?"

"It . . . just happened."

"I want to go home. I want to go back and see Cubby and Maxi."

"Dad's gone into the city. You'd be alone."

"I'll have the cats. Anything's better than this. Mum, I want to die, too."

"Now then, pet, what's all this about?" said Mrs Mallon. Alison looked round and saw her standing there, tactfully screening Alison from the children that were beginning to pile into school, even though Alison hadn't heard the bell. Mrs Mallon offered her a packet of paper tissues. Mrs Mallon was a teacher who stood no nonsense in class, but was wise enough to spot distress a long way off and quick to soothe it.

"This is the worst bit, Alison, pet. It'll be better once you're inside."

"That's what my Mum just said."

The teacher gave the girl a strange look, then shrugged and moved into cheerful overdrive, putting her arm across Alison's shoulders and steering her to the school door.

Inside was light, noise and bustle, wrapped in the scent of lavender furniture polish. Mrs Mallon showed her where to find her locker and peg. Alison was surprised to find them already labelled with her name. That helped, somehow. Then the teacher, arm still across shoulders, led her into the noisy classroom. Alison was staggered: everyone in the room snapped to attention behind his or her desk and silence fell with the speed of a camera shutter. She thought of her classrooms down South, where silence never fell even though hoarse teachers begged for it twenty times a day. Mrs Mallon stood with Alison at the front of the class, facing them all. She began to talk, and as she did, Alison found herself relaxing. The lump began to grow smaller in her throat, her tummy stopped clenching. She looked around at the faces that were looking at her. She saw no malice there. Instead, she saw curiosity, interest. She realised that she was a novelty and that her novelty was her strength. New pupils were rare here, she guessed. She represented a break in routine, a new ingredient of daily life, a source of possibilities. She relaxed a little more. She realised how small the class was: thirteen counting her. At her last school there had been nearly forty in her form.

"... from Hertfordshire, near London. Alison went to a big comprehensive there, lots more teachers and children than we've got and I should think life was a lot different for her. So you think what it would be like for you, if any of you were starting in Alison's old school. I know it'd flummox me. I might not be able to understand them and it'd take me ages to learn everyone's name. So let's imagine what it's like for Alison and try to show her we're not all heathens up here, eh? Now, get your Maths course ready for after Assembly. Alison, you sit over here ..."

And after that, it wasn't so bad at all.

"So what was it like?" asked Dad that afternoon, brewing tea and making toast in the kitchen.

"Not so bad, really. Didn't like the bus, though."

"Well, I'm not driving you there and back every day. It's potty. It's only a mile or two away. What's wrong with the bus anyway?"

49

"It picks up kids from other schools and they started making fun of my accent."

"What did you do about it?"

"My friends stuck up for me. There was nearly a punch-up."

"Your friends! Lordy Moses, you don't waste time, do you?"

There were five of them, but already she thought of Edith, the big boned farmer's daughter, and little Maisie as her special first-day friends. Maisie lived with her aunt and uncle in another village because her parents were in Saudi Arabia for two years. Edith's Dad farmed the land that swept up to the Coal House woods. She and Maisie had settled Alison into the school's routine, navigated her through the lunch break and huddled with her in the playground. They were fascinated by Alison's accent, as she by theirs. They unleashed a bounding pack of questions about Alison's previous life, school, loves, preferences, clothes, home, parents.

"My Mum's dead. I just live with me Dad."

An awkward pause. Mums didn't die. Not yet, anyway. Alison took on a new dimension of intrigue.

"What's your Dad do, like?"

Alison thought of him, sitting among his books in the room he had turned into a study, wearing his old white polo neck sweater, hunched over his typewriter, pecking away, stopping, reading, thinking, pecking, smoking.

"He's a typist."

They screamed with laughter. The girls wanted to pursue the point but an interruption headed them off. Swinging across the playground came Tommy Saddler. He stopped in front of the group of girls, a red-haired, freckled, cheeky chunk in a donkey jacket too small for him, faded jeans with brighter blue patches and a pullover with unashamed holes.

"Haway kiddo," he said to Alison and blew a gum bubble. "How's the Lady of the Manor, then? Got any more bunnies?"

"Two, actually. Not nearly enough." She felt a need to

50

make her new friends laugh and adopted a haughty voice: "And if I catch you poaching in the grounds without permission, I'll have you thrashed within an inch of your life and shipped straight to the Colonies."

The girls didn't laugh. Instead, Tommy Saddler regarded Alison directly for a few moments, his jaws chomping on the gum. Suddenly, he stopped chewing.

"Yeah," he said and walked away.

There was a silence. Alison found the others looking at her and, conspiratorially, from one to the other among themselves.

Edith said, "You know Tommy Saddler?"

Maisie said, "How d'you know him, like?"

Alison explained and they eased off, as if Alison were not to blame for a major social error.

"He's nae good at all, that one," said Maisie, wrinkling a pretty nose.

"My Dad chases him off the farm unless he's doing rabbits by request, like. My Dad says he pinches tatties and all sorts."

"He drowns kittens for people. In poly bags. With bricks. In the Beck."

"He's got ferrets."

Alison wasn't too clear what having ferrets involved, but it sounded like a contagious disease the way Edith said it. The conversation moved on and Alison was left with a feeling that the Tommy Saddler episode had, in some way, boosted her credit even further. It seemed unusual for anyone to associate with the lad and unheard of for a complete newcomer to have made his acquaintance so quickly. She thought of the early morning rabbit skins. She'd have to be careful.

After tea, Dad and Alison stood on the balcony, looking out at a roseate evening sky.

"Got any homework?"

"Not yet. They're still sorting me out. I've been doing

51

different things, like."

"You're picking up the accent already!"

"I am certainly not!"

"Do you mind if I pop over to the pub for half an hour? Ought to show my face from time to time. Integrate. Socialize."

"You mean booze."

"That as well. An elegant sufficiency, no more."

"It's illegal to leave a child unattended."

"It's a long time since you were a child. So you tell me. And anyway, the circumstances we find ourselves in, my old Al, it'll have to happen from time to time." He became serious and touched her shoulder. "I wouldn't if I felt I couldn't rely on you, you know."

"Oughtn't you to be working?"

"Done a lot today. Let the labourer rest."

"Oh all right, then," she said, tossing her hair in mock disgust. "Leave me, walk away, go boozing with the miners, go and mix with fallen women, get sloshed, gamble our lives away while I sit here alone, warming my hands by the starving cats, deserted."

"I knew you'd understand."

He lit an unnecessary but nice log fire and she settled down with Cubby and Max to put in some serious telly-watching.

He walked up the drive, hearing a rising wind roar in the treetops and noting the potholes that he'd have to fill in. He couldn't tell how much of a success school had been, but it certainly hadn't been a disaster. His relief was immense. He'd been worrying about it more than he admitted to himself: worry was always worse when it was necessary to demonstrate that you weren't worried at all. He supposed he ought to join the PTA. He'd had a letter. He'd always left that to her, the wifely duty which she'd done so well, baking cakes and manning stalls, attending meetings and running sports days. Though he remembered her once saying how boring she found it, she did it. He'd make the effort. Ye gods.

52

Outside the pub's front door was a wind trap. From whichever direction the wind blew, it ended by swirling and snatching at the arriving or departing customers. He ducked through it and into the Public Bar.

It was a big room, with high, stuccoed ceiling and stark, cream walls. The bar was massive and sprouted beer pumps and illuminated plastic fonts. A log and coal fire burned in a modern fireplace, in front of which dreamed a labrador bitch. Piped music was blessedly faint but annoyingly tinny.

The place was almost empty. The strike had robbed it of customers. A man of about sixty sat beside the fire, sipping brown ale and rolling cigarettes by hand. Two youths played darts at the far end of the room. A smartly dressed middle aged couple played silent dominoes on a square blackboard laid upon a table. A man in postman's uniform played the one-arm bandit with steady concentration and occasional success. There was nobody behind the bar.

He waited.

"You'd best ring the bell, bonny lad," said the old man by the fireside. "Ye'll be here till midnight, else."

He found a brass bar-bell, shaped like a Regency lady with a crinoline. It tinkled loudly.

"Aye, she's the only woman I know with a clapper under her skirt, like," said the man by the fire and wheezed with laughter.

A pleasant-faced woman with grey hair and crinkly eyes appeared from the depths of the pub and served him with a pint of beer. On impulse, he ordered a packet of crisps, not because he was peckish, but because he couldn't believe that any crisp could genuinely taste of the mixture of flavours advertised on the packet. He was right.

The landlady returned to the back of the pub, where Alec could just see a sedate Lounge Bar and Restaurant. He perched on a bar stool, crunched crisps and sipped beer. He took stock.

There was something wrong. No, not wrong, simply not right. He felt a dislocation, bumpy under the surface of daily life. On that surface, everything seemed to be better than he could have hoped. The house was in shape now. Work was sticky, but work always stuck. Alison was settling. Peter was tilling the soil with an expensive vengeance. Financial arrangements, though complex beyond his reckoning, seemed to be holding up. Why did he have a feeling of being followed, watched, judged? He took the various elements of their life and prodded them to discover the culprit.

After a while, he told himself that there were two, but he couldn't decide why or how they were causing his unease. One was the countryside. He remembered his first response when he drove into the enclave of reclaimed coalfield. It had deepened with familiarity. It was as if the land had been savaged beyond support and hastily patched up, a surgery that had not quite succeeded. Topsoil and grass seed were not enough to heal the old wounds.

And there was the Coal House.

That there was a presence in and around the house, apart from Alison and himself, he was certain, though he didn't know who or what it was. Each night, he waited up until he was reasonably sure that Alison was asleep before he went to his bedroom. There, he would read for a while, perhaps drink a nightcap of hot whisky and turn out the light to lie awake and think about his wife and his life until sleep rescued him. It was then, watching the black night beyond the open curtains and listening to the roar of wind in the sycamores that he had, on several occasions, been aware of someone or something outside in the gardens or in the woods. Nothing he could hear. When he got up and peered out, nothing he could see. A clear impression, nevertheless, of a watchful presence. Not even that, but a presence that moved and had being. Sometimes he would feel it away among the far trees. Then, after a few minutes, he would know that it was behind him, at the front of the house. A little later, by the greenhouse. Later still, he would be convinced that it had gone.

Once, he had pulled on some jeans and a sweater, taken a flashlight and gone for a walk right round the house and grounds. Apart from bouncing the beam of his light from the amazed pupils of Cubby and Max, he had seen nothing. Unless those marks in the wet grass had been made by the passage of feet? Unless Alison had left the gate open after he had closed and latched it? Perhaps that croak in the woods was only an owl, after all?

It was not an exclusively night feeling. Working at home, he often escaped from the study to brew tea and pace the house or garden. On one such jaunt, he came across some freshly turned earth in the orchard. Peter, obviously. Only an hour or so later did he remember that Peter had not been for two days and had limited himself to the vegetable garden and greenhouse. Animals? What animals? No young cats could remove old and solid turves. Foxes? If so, why there? On another occasion he found a ragged scrap of black cloth on the barbed wire fence beside the farmer's field. It had not been there the previous day. He knew because it was one of his favoured pausing places, with a view down to the city and cathedral and a seductive scent of wild garlic from the matted undergrowth. She had loved wild garlic. Its subtle smell brought back summers they had tasted together. The piece of black cloth felt stiff. He was reminded of a cassock or a cloak.

He was quietly sure of all this. Since she had died, he had been able to consider himself from outside in a way he never needed to when she was with him and they could share ideas of who one another was. He was not hag-ridden. He had no time for ghosties and ghoulies. He put a high value on instinct and emotion but superstition had no place in his life. Whatever the explanation, it was exactly that: explicable in ordinary terms, without recourse to mumbo jumbo.

"Are ye from the Coal House, like?"

The man from the fireside was beside him, tinkling the crinoline for more brown ale. Alec started.

"I'm sorry, I was miles away. Yes. Moved in last week."

"Aye, I thought so. I'm Geordie Harrison. Nice to see the place with people again."

Alec introduced himself, bought the brown ale, though he was as sure as he could be that he wasn't being touched for

55

it, refilled his pint glass, discarded the crisps and joined Geordie by the fireside. Almost immediately, Geordie began to contribute to Alec's considerations.

Geordie had known the Coal House since his childhood, some sixty years ago. He talked of village fetes on the lawn, immaculate driveways, carriages and fours kept on from Victorian days, limousines, chauffeurs, teams of gardeners and female relatives 'in service'. Alec found Geordie good company, a cheerful man with a wickedly realistic sense of humour that sparkled through the mist of a lifetime of brown ales. Alec Lucas decided to chance his arm.

"Are there ghost stories about the place? Is it haunted?"

Geordie chortled. "Not that I know of, man, though the buggers that have lived there, you'd think the place was standing-room only with tormented souls by now."

The older man paused and seemed to remember something unexpectedly. Turning towards Alec he said, "Hey, wait now. There's some old photographs of your place. Have you seen 'em at all?"

"No. I'd very much like to." Alec was interested.

"Aye, canny old photographs they are, nineteen hundred and thereabouts. I couldn't say who had them in the first place, like, but the landlord before this one kept them behind the bar for years. They could still be there. He was always going to frame them, you see, for the posh bar, but he were an idle sod and never did. Just wait there, bonny lad."

Geordie waddled to the bar and used the crinoline bell to summon the landlady. He asked about the photographs, but she was uncertain.

"I'll ask Harry."

After some ten minutes and another pint, Harry the landlord appeared with an old, brown envelope which bulged fatly. He joined them by the fire and was formally introduced to Alec by Geordie Harrison. Alec had a feeling of acceptance that he found comforting. Inside the envelope was a thick wadge of old photographs, some sepia, some black and white, sometimes mounted on thick board or in

56

frayed wallets, often single postcards, creased and fingered. There were pictures of the village when the pits were in full production, portraits of villagers lined up by a charabanc for the annual outing to the coast, pictures of the Institute, a handsome building now long gone. The original collector had clearly been a keen sportsman: the village cricket and football teams were represented, from the turn of the century well into the nineteen fifties. Sombre men with moustaches and long shorts glared fiercely at the camera on sunlit afternoons. And there were photographs of the Coal House.

"Trouble is," said Alec, "I've really been out too long. The daughter's on her own and I shouldn't leave her any longer."

"Why, he can take them with him can't he, Harry?"

"Don't see why not, mind."

"Thanks. Thanks very much. Alison'll be fascinated. I'll take good care of them. Bring them back tomorrow."

"No rush, man. You might be able to get copies made, in town."

The wind was even noisier above the driveway on the walk home. The trees thrashed and creaked. He wondered how often one came down; there was a fallen sycamore beyond, in the woods, the gash in its trunk comparatively recent.

"You took your time. Poo, you pong of beer."

"Sorry. Good reason, though. Look . . ."

He spread the photographs on the carpet in front of the fire. At this point he noticed something about Alison's behaviour. She was still, it seemed, determined not to show too much enthusiasm over matters concerning the Coal House: she needed to show Dad that this enforced captivity in the bleak North was none of her choosing and that she was suffering nobly through it. At the same time, the magic of old photographs obviously affected her, so that she was torn between an offhand, mild disinterest and a desire to peer closely into the unusual past.

Dad picked up a postcard, a sepia photograph of what was

57

the true front of the house in 1900, the date on the written note on the postcard side. He read it aloud to Alison.

My dear Mary,
The weather stays fine and Mother seems much
better. We are planning a day by the sea tomorrow,
and I may be back by Friday. Send for me sooner if
you need me. Yours, A.

"Who's it addressed to?"
"Miss M. Keenlyside, Church Avenue, in the city. Sounds like sisters, one visiting their Mum, maybe."
" 'A' might be a man."
"Doesn't sound like one, somehow. June 14th, 1900. The house must have been something then, to warrant having postcards made of it."
"They used to call it 'The Castle'."
"How d'you know that?"
"Mrs Mallon told us. She was a little girl in the village. Before the war."
Alison had clearly shown too much interest and busied herself stroking Cubby and Max, who were tied in a sleepy knot on an armchair. Dad inspected the postcard.
The photograph had been taken from the main lawn, straight on to the house frontage. The white verandah was pristine, roller blinds half drawn at all the windows, paintwork gleaming. The drive, now overgrown, was a sweep of immaculate pea gravel, circling up to the front door. The gardens were neat and formal, the circle inside the driveway decorated with shrubs, a border of flowers on either side of the front door, an auracaria tree to one side of the house.
"What's that?"
"Monkey puzzle tree. Gone now."
He was fascinated to see how little the sycamore trees had changed. They looked as big in the photographs as they did now, but that was impossible. If they were fully grown now, they would be barely half grown when the photographer set up his tripod and Victoria was still Queen of England. He

determined to take the photograph out with him in daylight and make a careful comparison.

Then he saw it.

The balcony on the verandah was side lit by an afternoon sun, he guessed about three o'clock on a summer's day. Part in shadow, part in light, the french windows that led out of the master bedroom and on to the balcony were a patchwork of sepia shades. The white roller blinds had been neurotically positioned, precisely half way down each window. He could even make out the dangling cords with their tasselled bobbles. And he could make out more than that.

In the left hand window, just catching the slanting sunlight, was a face. It was peeping round the corner of the window, as if it should not have been there but could not resist watching the photographer on the lawn. The face was low down, near the sill: either a child or a crouching adult. He looked again and compared the size of the face with the dimensions of the window frame. A child, almost definitely.

The face was indistinct. It was far away from the camera, behind glass and probably held back, away from the tell-tale window. Even so, Dad could make out long hair and a white garment, high on the neck.

"Ally," he said, "you're not the only young lady who's lived in the Coal House."

And he showed her the portrait of a young girl on a summer's day, spying on the photographer from her parents' bedroom window.

She knew she should not be there, of course. Father would be very stand-offish if he knew. Mother would scold. Yet this was a singular day, and she would regret forever not seeing what was happening on the lawn. Nevertheless, the instructions had been clear: "The house, Mister Marks, simply the house to be portrayed, with the gardens. No people whatsoever. Our family and staff shall not appear in a commercial portrayal. The house, alone, sir."

And Mister Marks, the photographer from the city shop had bowed, agreed and fixed a date, "subject, naturally, to climatic suitability".

She had seen photographic apparatus before, naturally. On or around her birthday each year she was taken to be portrayed by Mister Marks in his dusty studio high above the old city. She hated it. Her head was clamped to the back of a chair and she was cajoled into holding foolish objects, such as sprays of paper flowers, bowls of wax fruit or an improving book. Once, they had wanted her to dress in a white robe and lean against a Grecian column. She had cried and the photographic sitting had been cancelled.

She tried to forget those torture sessions, but elements of them stayed, infuriatingly, in her mind. Mainly smells: the pervasive smell of boiled mutton from Mister Marks' rooms above the studio; the musty, crackly smell of his black, stiff hood underneath which he crouched while busying himself with the camera; the oily scent given off by the canvas backcloth upon which was painted a hazy, sylvan landscape, against which all the notaries of the city and all the spoiled children had, at one time or another, been depicted in soft tones of ochre and sepia. She remembered, too, the clack of hooves outside the studio, skittering on the tarwood blocks of the steep streets, and the hollow boom of the nearby Cathedral bells.

Today, there was silence except for birdsong and a whisper of breeze in the sycamores. She felt safe. Mister Marks was no longer on his smelly home territory but there, outside on the lawn, fumbling and no doubt perspiring in his heavy business clothes. It was a hot, sunlit afternoon, crowded with butterflies and alive with midges. A blackbird was singing in the auracaria tree.

The servants had been confined to the house for an hour, her father was away at one of the pits and her mother was sewing in the drawing room. She was alone at the front of the house and slowly moving forward to peep round the window frame, underneath the half drawn blind.

There he was, a black hump in the middle of the lawn.

He looked exactly like a giant insect with a humped carapace and five legs, three for the tripod, two for Mister Marks. One circular eye stared at the house from the folds of black, unblinking as it drank in the forms of the building. Was he making a photograph now? Would she be seen by that eye? She crouched motionless, sure that if she did not move, she would not be noticed by the insect.

The scene, though intriguingly unusual, was motionless. She grew bored quickly and her eyes wandered over the grounds, beyond the still photographer. She drew her breath sharply and held it. In front of the far hedge, which separated the lawn from the orchard, stood another figure. Tall, also in black, wearing a cloak and a wide brimmed hat, it – for she did not know whether it was a man or a woman – it looked steadily up at the house without moving. The cloak reached right to the grass and the face was in shadow, the sunlight streaming from behind and shattered by the hedge. She searched inside herself to determine who it could be. She failed to find an answer. She knew nobody who dressed like that and she did not believe she knew anybody that tall. Minutes passed. None of the three figures in the scene moved an inch. The blackbird, unconcerned, sang from the monkey puzzle tree.

Suddenly, there came a sense of conclusion from beneath the insect-hood and Mister Marks emerged, straightening and rubbing his back. The sudden movement seemed wrong in that photographically still landscape. When she looked past the insect, the other black figure had disappeared. Or did she see the tail of a black cloak swing through the orchard gateway? She could not be sure, but the black watcher must have moved on the instant that Mister Marks came out from his hood, almost as if anticipating the very second it would happen.

She saw Mister Marks stretch and look behind him for several moments, as if he too had heard a movement or felt a presence. Then he carefully began to dismantle his apparatus and stow it in walnut cases on the lawn.

The episode was over. It left a lasting impression in the

girl's mind, just as the sunlight filtering through the insect's eye left an image on the glass plate behind it that would echo down the years until it met Alison and her Dad.

As the girl left her parents' bedroom, the blackbird in the puzzle tree saw a movement down in the orchard and flew, chattering, away to the safety of the sycamores.

Chapter 6

As the school term decayed with the spring, weather patterns right round the planet shuffled, swirled and settled down for a summer that was going to be remembered for years by sunlovers all over Europe.

Alec and Alison Lucas saw their first summer in the Coal House as a slow dance from chaos to a kind of order. With Peter Robson's help, the jungle-garden was levelled, tidied, cut, fed, watered. Fruit bushes began to promise buckets of berries. Small, green apples appeared and, in the greenhouse, tomato plants swarmed and filled the air with their smoky scents. Dad ripened like the fruit, growing browner and brighter, fascinated by the novelty of growing his own food and working at the land.

"I don't know what we're going to live on if you don't stop pottering with Peter and do some work."

"Neither do I, Ally. But ain't Life grand!"

Alison's grudge against the move North was still there, to be brought out and dusted down occasionally. But for most of the time it was overlaid by her enjoyment of the summer, and the times she spent with her new friends. Edith, stolid, dismissive of childishness. Maisie, twinkling and bouncing, with a devilishly well-informed sense of humour. Alison's Southern strangeness to them both served her well: the three girls intrigued one another equally.

On the last day of summer term, they stayed late at school to help Mrs Mallon tidy up the room. Mrs Mallon, too, had been a comfort. Alison was well aware of the extra time spent on her, the watchful check on her moods and manner after that first day.

They were unpinning charts from the pinboards. Edith was taking down the term's drawings, Maisie was collecting drawing pins and putting them in a plastic margarine pot, Alison was helping Mrs Mallon with the three, very big wildlife posters that were stuck on a side wall. One showed pictures of "Common British Birds", another "Small Mammals of Field and Woodland" and the third, "Our Favourite Pets".

"Bit childish really," said Mrs Mallon, stretching from a desktop and grunting.

"Say that again," moaned Edith. "We had one of them at Infants, like."

"One of those."

"No, one of *them*."

"Edith . . ."

"S'all right, I know. Really."

Mrs Mallon was having trouble reaching the topmost pins. Alison, inexplicably taller than she had ever been before, persuaded the panting teacher to let her take over. With relief, Mrs Mallon argued not at all, but went and sat at her own desk and lit a naughty cigarette, watching the three girls. She liked them. She knew the rules about having favourites and blissfully ignored them.

"If you were a bird on that chart, what bird would you be?" she said suddenly.

"Sparrowhawk," from Maisie, immediately.

"Oh heck," said Edith. "Magpie, I suppose. No, four magpies."

"Why?"

" 'One for sorrow, two for joy, like, three for a girl and four for a boy.' See?"

Mrs Mallon didn't.

"She wants a boyfriend," said Alison, offhandedly.

"And what would you be, if you were a bird?"

"Oh, an owl. Then I could hunt at night. Stay up late."

Mrs Mallon was bored with birds. Alison was taking down the "Small Mammals" poster. They started nominating animals for themselves. Edith, the farmer's daughter, wisely chose to be a mole, which kept well clear of combine harvesters, ploughs and chemicals and slept safely underground. Maisie tittered and wanted to be a mouse as long as there weren't any cats around. This made Alison think about being Cubby or Max, but she remembered the strong smell of their food when she opened the tin every morning and opted to be a rabbit instead. She knew she was influenced by past delights: pictures in story books of cuddly bunnies, dressed in mob caps and aprons, busily bustling round warrens that were inexplicably furnished with chintz, pine dressers and china teapots.

She also knew that in one of the Coal House stables were twenty five cleaned and scraped rabbit pelts. The knowledge didn't change her decision.

A little later, the three girls were walking up the road towards the village. They paused at the lane which led to Edith's farm. Arrangements were loosely made for meetings, outings, swimming trips, shopping sprees in the city. Nothing was definite, summer gaped ahead, school shrank behind. They would meet up, but the details were unimportant for now. The sky was a milky purple, the sun still high over the faraway Cathedral tower. The countryside sweated with summer.

Through the hedge by which they stood were the allotments where Tommy shot rabbits. Beyond the allotments, on the far side of the far hedge, was Tommy. Between the girls and Tommy was a fine buck rabbit.

They didn't hear the crack of the air rifle: it was just another, faint and unconsidered noise of a summer afternoon which popped with heat and life. Edith and Maisie both heard Alison's squeal as she clapped her hand to her cheek and spun away from them. She stumbled and fell to her knees. Blood glittered on her fingers and tears shone in her eyes. They dropped their satchels and knelt to help her. Tommy Saddler appeared at the farm lane's entrance, staring at them across the road. Edith looked up and nudged Maisie.

"You little bastard!" yelled Maisie. "You've shot her!"

The doctor at the city hospital managed to avoid the use of stitches. He prised the pellet from Alison's cheek, using a local anaesthetic. All that Alison felt was a grubbing about and a sudden easing of tension. An immaculate dressing was applied and Dad drove her home. Her face felt fat and silent, her right eye watered a little.

"You'll be OK."

"Scarred for life and he says I'll be OK."

"Ally, you won't be scarred. It'll heal nicely."

"Scarface Lucas, that'll be me from now on."

"Shush. No harm done."

Tommy Saddler could have benefited from the conversation. When it was taking place, he was sitting alone in the garden shed, staring at the closed door and waiting for the police to come and arrest him, as they surely would. He was so miserable and so frightened that he spoke aloud.

"What a pillock."

In a delicate situation, Tommy could usually be expected to behave well. He had a wary wisdom well in advance of his years. When he realised that he had shot Alison in the face, the wisdom had left him.

He had run away.

That this was stupid, useless and incriminating, he knew full well, even as he pounded up the field path, the pellet tin castanetting in his pocket, the rifle thumping his back and his breath lurching out in great sobs. Nevertheless, he had to get away, as far away as possible, from the horror of what he'd done. Or what he *thought* he'd done: for the last Tommy had seen was a girl lying on the ground, blood coming from what he suspected was her eye, trickling through her fingers as her friends knelt and fussed. She might be blind.

She would be blind.

66

She was, certainly, blind. By him.

He had to get away. As he neared the top of the field, it came to him how little scope he had for escape. There was the village and the village and the village. There was nowhere else. What he'd done, he'd have to pay for.

He stopped against the Coal House fence, sucking air in and hissing it out. Looking across the front lawn at the house, he saw a light in one of the ground floor rooms and saw Alison's Dad walk across a room, lighting a cigarette and looking at his watch. Tommy climbed the fence and walked as steadily as he was able to the front door. As he hammered the brass knocker, it occurred to Tommy that he had no idea how an educated, soft-spoken Southerner would react to what he was to announce.

"Hello Tommy. Been rabbiting yet again?"

"Mister Lucas."

"Yes?"

"Mister Lucas."

"Well?"

"I've just, like, shot Alison. In the eye. With this. By accident."

Later, Tommy could never remember what filled the moments between his announcement and the shriek of car tyres on the gravel as Alison's Dad sped off to find his daughter, leaving Tommy desolate by the door. There had been an explosion of rapid, specific questions which had flustered Tommy and frustrated Lucas. There had been the sour smell of panic, adult panic. There had been the banging of doors, the squawl from the garage hinges, the roar of the car and the grating yell as it slewed round and away up the drive. Then there was nothing but the afternoon sunlight and Tommy, alone with his rifle.

He carried it home. Without entering his house, he slid down the side passage, into the garden and shut himself in the shed to prepare himself for the coming of the police. The shed smelled of dust, wood, oil, paraffin and ferrets, who scrambled uncaring in their cages. Tommy found the same, unworthy thought recurring:

"If I had to get in bad, why did it have to be the first day of the holidays?"

Forcing himself to be less selfish, he thought of Alison. He closed one eye and squinted at the fly-smeared window, trying to imagine blindness. The other eye pricked with tears. He was done for.

He judged it to be around eight in the evening when he heard a car stop outside the house: the last light was fading from the summer sky, the shed was close and gloomy. He heard their silly door chimes, then the sound of men's voices. Mister Lucas and his Dad. Tommy winced: it was his Dad who sounded angry, not Alison's Dad. Footsteps. A car door. The car driving away, turning and heading back towards the drive to the Coal House. Then the kitchen door opening to the garden. Tommy's stomach tilted. Nevertheless, he stood, went to the shed door, unhitched it and opened it. His Dad filled the doorframe. He looked white and sweaty, as if he had just recovered from a shock.

In a surprisingly, scarily quiet voice, his Dad told him that Alison was going to be all right and her father was not going to involve the police, though by rights he should and had every good reason.

"He asked me to have a good talk to you, instead. So come on, you little bugger."

That night Tommy went to sleep on his front, his back, buttocks and legs a zebra crossing of weals from his Dad's leather's belt. There had been just one consolation to the whole miserable business.

He had been ordered to go and work in the Coal House garden, unpaid, for as long as Mister Lucas wanted some things done.

So, at least, he could return to the Coal House. See Alison. Shoot rabbits. He hoped Mister Lucas wanted lots done.

That same evening, Alison's Dad sat on the balcony with his whisky, watching the stars in a steadily purpling sky. Far behind in the house was the sound of a pop cassette playing in Alison's bedroom. He looked for his wife in the evening but she had not come. He wondered if that was because, in the heart-stopping shock of hearing about his daughter's accident he had become, for once, a total parent. In the old days, he would have been at work. Helen would have heard the news, dashed to help, driven to the hospital, suffered the worry. He would only have heard about it when he came home. He would have been angry, sympathetic, relieved, but it would all be secondhand stuff compared to the flood of agony that had drowned him when the Saddler urchin had calmly informed him his daughter had been shot through the eye. The little swine. If the boy's father kept his word and sent the lad over to help out around the place, by God he'd find some mucky work for him to do.

Dad found himself looking down on the lawn and thinking that he must be seeing it almost from the same angle as the little girl in the old photograph. More than eighty years ago she had peeped through the window just behind his shoulder and looked down on the immaculate, sunlit lawn. Now it was deep in summer shadow, unkempt and unstocked. He wondered if the late Victorian girl had stayed on, grown up and become an Edwardian Lady of the House. She would be dead now.

What if Alison were dead now, killed this afternoon? Dad swallowed whisky and wrenched his mind away on a different route. The Victorian girl. He wondered if it would be possible to find out more about her, to uncover the history of the Coal House and its succession of occupants. Helen had always been keen on "projects" for Alison during the long summer break. Mind, Dad thought ruefully, few of them were ever a complete success or even completed. There had been the weather chart summer: plastic bottles collecting rain all over the garden, a home-made wind vane that kept blowing over. Then there had been the summer of the bird-count. In the kitchen had hung a chart of brightly coloured wild birds, chaffinches, tits, fieldfares, robins, magpies. Beside each bird was a square for Alison to keep a tally of average sightings in the garden. At the end of the summer, the tally had been one robin five times and nothing else except a numbing score of five hundred and seventy six sparrows and three hundred and two starlings. Oh yes, and one escaped budgie from next door but one. Dad smiled.

An owl cried in the trees. He thought to himself: "A bird count would be spectacular here. But she probably wouldn't wear it a second time." The history of the Coal House was something quite different. He'd like to know more himself. He began to think up a list of useful sources of information.

Next morning at breakfast, Alison warmed to the idea. Secretly she was hoping to unearth a local history book in the library and short circuit all the research but even so she had a genuine interest in what had gone on in the house over the years.

"Going to bike in to the library, then?"

"Not today. Not yet."

He saw her touch the bulky dressing on her cheek and realised she was self conscious about it. There was time.

Things got moving when Edith and Maisie both went on holiday at the same time, one to Spain, the other to Cornwall, leaving Alison behind and bored.

"Dad, why can't we go on holiday?"

"Can't afford it this year, lovey, spent all me loot on this place. Anyway, I've got two textbooks to write by September."

On a warm, overcast day, she cycled to the nearest library, adopted her best serious-student manner, enlisted the help of the librarian and came away with a book on the history of the coalfield and a village-by-village guide to the county which looked promising. She spent the afternoon with them, and, by foraging through indexes, managed to get several pages of useful notes. For his part, Dad took to jotting down odd remarks made by Peter, Geordie Harrison and Harry at the pub. Billy the milkman proved a valuable source of information. His family had been supplying milk to the area for several generations. Even Billy remembered riding the horse-drawn cart as a lad, dispensing ladles of milk from a swishing churn.

"One ladle for half a pint, one for a pint, one for a quart. And we always added a little slosh 'for the cat', see?"

But the most unexpected provider of historical detail was Tommy Saddler.

One afternoon, the boy had been set to repairing a paling fence at the edge of the woods. He worked uncomplainingly, dressed in patched jeans, old trainers and a holey sweater, with a tiny transistor radio for company. Alison was sitting in the kitchen, her notes spread out on the shelf when Dad came in to brew up coffee. Together they watched the distant figure of the boy as he straightened uprights and renailed crosspieces. The sky had been towering with ragged cloud canyons all afternoon and it suddenly split open, hurling rain straight down with such force that it bounced back from every hard surface it found. Tommy scampered for the shelter of a sycamore. Lightning burned across the garden, thunder deafeningly on its tail.

"Hey Dad, he'll get struck. Or drowned. You can't leave him out there."

Dad went to the kitchen door and called to him. Through the curtains of rain came Tommy, bedraggled and running fast, his transistor tucked under his sweater. He ducked into the kitchen and stood on the mat, creating lagoons of water at his feet.

"Aye, that's a bugger, that one."

Dad regarded Tommy suspiciously. He supposed the lad had served his punishment by now, if punishment it was: yet Tommy continued to turn up, uncomplaining, and worked long and steadily at whatever task he was given. Dad, ignoring Peter's sniffy remarks, found the boy very helpful.

"Cup of tea? Or a cold drink?"

"Why aye, thanks."

As the thunderstorm clattered outside, they drank ginger beer. Tommy sneaked a peek over Alison's shoulder.

"Chadoin'?"

She told him. Tommy grinned and said:

"You want to talk to me Grandad. He's crazy for history,

71

like. He'd fettle all that for you."

"Where's he live?"

"With us. But he never comes downstairs. His legs. Got his own room, too, the old bugger. Piled high with maps and old papers and that. I'll bring you some if you like. If he'll lend them. He's a bit jealous of them, you see. But I'll work on him. He needs me to get his tabs from the pub. I could threaten to stop supplies."

The threat worked. Next day Tommy arrived at the Coal House early in the morning carrying a cardboard grocery box filled with papers, neatly folded and kept in dogeared, labelled manilla envelopes. There were old footpath, boundary and parish maps, back copies of the local newspaper stretching well back into the nineteenth century, individual cuttings and old parish magazines.

"Keep them in order and good nick," said Dad. "The old boy's obviously been collecting them all his life."

"He's eighty-one," said Tommy proudly, "and he says he got a lot of this junk from his own Dad, like, so that's going back a bit."

Tommy, uninterested in paperwork, waited to be given a job to do in the damp garden, but Dad relented and, spotting the fact that the boy had his rifle with him, allowed him to go rabbiting in the woods.

"Just make sure rabbits are all you shoot."

Tommy squirmed and looked at Alison who looked calmly back at him. The scar had almost faded from her cheek. Slowly, on the side farthest from Dad, Alison winked at Tommy, who grinned. He knew now that the whole business was over and went off to the woods with a lighter heart than he'd known for weeks. Alison dived into the old papers and Dad went off to the study.

It was nearly lunchtime when there came a squeal from the kitchen. Dad raced through the house, visions of more pellet wounds before his eyes. Alison was on her way to fetch him and they collided in the dining room.

"What is it?"

"I've found it, I'm sure I have. It's awfully sad."

72

She spread an old, yellow newspaper on the dining table. It was much bigger than the modern tabloid paper, with a front page crammed with boxed and ruled advertisements and notices, the name of the newspaper in solid black gothic type. Dad saw the date was in September, 1900. Alison, with the air of a conjuror, peeled back the front page and pointed to an item on page three. It was in the column headed Obituaries, under the name of the village.

> Quietly, in her sleep, MARTHA ELEANOR PATTEN, only daughter of George and Elizabeth, at the Colliery Manager's House, aged thirteen years and eleven months. Private interment at Saint Lawrence Church.
>
> *Thus you go where we must follow,*
> *Sad to say you went ahead,*
> *So we wait for a glorious morrow*
> *When we meet, we sainted dead.*

"Bit gruesome, that."

"She was the same age as me. Awful, isn't it. Brings it home."

"And you think . . ."

"The girl in the photograph. It must be. They usd to call this the Colliery Manager's House before it got called the Coal House. Only daughter. Thirteen, nearly fourteen. And the newspaper's 1900, same year as the photograph. In fact, if the photograph was taken that summer, she only had a few more weeks to live."

Dad was looking at a news item elsewhere on the page. "Look at this. There was an influenza epidemic round the city. I wonder if that's what got her. It was a killer in those days, carried off kids and old people particularly. There was a big one after the First World War, too. Slaughtered millions."

"Dad, shush."

"Martha Eleanor Patten. Wonder if they called her Nellie. Poor little lass."

"Patten was Colliery Manager from 1891 to 1905, I think. I've made a list of them all from Tommy's Grandad's stuff. Well, nearly all, there are some gaps."

Dad went back to his work and Alison sat still, contemplating the long ago death of Martha Eleanor.

She was interrupted by Tommy Saddler knocking at the kitchen door. He was holding up a fresh rabbit pelt, brown with a silvery sheen.

Death was in the air.

There was an Indian Summer that year. September was still and hot, a parade of clear, blue days. Even so, they kept a fire burning in her bedroom night and day: the doctor advised it, to help her sweat the fever out of her body. The thick velvet curtains were usually drawn shut, making the room a hothouse.

She didn't care. She lay in the big bed, watching the walls of the room pulse and waver through her half-closed eyes. Her hair stuck to her forehead and neck, her skin burned and shivered. Sometimes she saw demons, fantastical figures that had escaped from her book of Grimms' Tales or from some over-enthusiastic cautionary tract handed out at Sunday School. They swam through the air and incorporated themselves in the shadowy wallpaper. Her toes played with a stone hot water jar under the bedclothes. There was a taste of bitter dust in her mouth and the sound of distant streams in her ears.

Her mother sat with her often and read to her as she dipped in and out of a restless sleep. The whole house behind and below her was unusually quiet: she did not know that the servants had been ordered to tiptoe and whisper. The doctor drove out from the city every day to see her and talked in hushed tones to her mother and father, something about "the crisis approaching" and "the crucial period". She wondered what a crisis was like and dozed off into brightly coloured nightmares.

Then, one day, when it seemed to her that she had been

74

in bed all summer, the fever flared up. All her senses switched off and she was aware of very little except, occasionally, her mother's face or a cool napkin on her forehead. She lay and trembled, soaked with sweat, listening to a strange voice saying silly, unrelated things and not recognising it as her own. Time passed, though she had no appreciation of how long the fever took.

Suddenly, she woke up and found the room empty. Firelight rippled and made dark corners. It was night. Her head was ringing with emptiness and she could feel every part of her body with an acute sensitivity. Most of all, she was cool, cooler than she had been for days. Deep inside her was a cave of pure ice, which expanded and contracted. Sometimes it seemed as if the ice would come right out through her skin, then it would shrink to a pinpoint above her stomach.

Very carefully, she folded back the heavy bedclothes and swung her feet out, round and down. They dangled above the carpet. She was exhausted, weak, but she managed to stand upright. She wobbled and swayed and the ice-cave boomed larger. Holding the bed, she took her first steps for two weeks, towards the dark velvet curtains. She realised that at some time she had been moved into her parents' room, though she could not remember being carried here.

There was a gap of several feet between the bed and the curtains which she had to manage without help. The ice grew in her as she tottered forward into space. She began to buckle at the knees, fell forward and clutched the thick velvet just in time. The ice was roaring outwards now and her chest was tightening. She slid through the curtains and stood in the cool cavern that lay between them and the balcony windows.

The lawn was swimming in moonlight, bright as day, the black shadows under the sycamores like velvet themselves. She leaned against the windows, tasting the cold glass with the tip of her tongue and watching her little breaths making misty spirals. Through the misty marks, she saw a movement outside. She wiped a patch clear and looked again.

Down by the hedge, where it had stood in the summer, was the figure in black. It was looking up at her and wrapping its black cloak closer around its body against the chilly moonlight. The wide black hat hid the face from her. She wondered if it was "the crisis" and if so, whether it would approach. But then she felt the ice cave blossom until it touched her skin and burst out from her body. She saw that her breath was no longer leaving mist on the glass. As she slid to the floor she knew who the black figure must be. Perhaps if she . . .

Chapter 7

On a Friday night in August, Alison saw men trying to kill one another and Alison's Dad went to a party.

"I won't be late," he said, putting on a tie for the first time that summer.

"Dirty stop-out," said Alison, brushing his jacket for him. "Don't come back drunk."

"Cheeky. It's not that sort of party, anyway. Very academic. Nigerian claret and mousetrap cheese, I bet."

"Who'd you say invited you?"

"A woman I met in the University Library when I was looking something up. She's a lecturer in English. Anyway, turns out she recognised my name from the textbooks . . ."

"Fame! Give her your autograph, did you?"

". . . and invited me along to this do of hers, meet some of her colleagues. Couldn't really get out of it."

"Go on. I bet you fancied her, or something."

She realised what she'd said and felt ashamed. She also realised that her Dad had, very slightly, blushed. He did not answer her but said instead:

"What's that do you said you were going to?"

"Oh, Edith's brother's twenty-first at the Village Hall. They're having a disco and everything. Edith says me and Maisie can help her Mum with the buffet."

"Maisie and I."

"Suit yourself, but it's hardly your scene, dear."

God, these flashes of regression into childishness took

him more and more by surprise the fewer they became. He ignored it.

"How you getting down and back?"

"It's only a mile. Walk down with Maisie, walk back too, if Edith's Dad doesn't give us a lift. Hope he does. He's got a Land Rover."

Alison's Dad, looking, she thought, remarkably neat and tidy, climbed into the car and drove off through a cloudy evening towards the city. As she watched the car slip away through the trees, Alison had a passing feeling that something important was going to happen. She had no idea what it might be or to whom it might happen, but there was a fleeting sense of momentousness in the evening air. Then she saw a movement in the drive and thought Dad was coming back for some reason. It was Maisie, bouncy and still brown from Cornwall.

"Ee, aren't you ready yet? Gerramoveon, girl."

Alison raided the fridge for a cola, which Maisie swigged from the can while Alison squeezed into her tight jeans, a crocheted sweater and a silver bomber jacket that her Dad loathed. She applied some make-up. She was quietly proud of her touch in the make-up department. Edith never bothered, Maisie usually went too far, but Alison had developed blusher, eye-shadow and lip gloss to a state of art whereby she looked and felt good and Dad rarely noticed she was wearing the stuff at all. She raided her money box for small change and two pound coins, which she wriggled into her back pocket. Then they were off, Alison locking the door and hanging the key round her neck beneath her sweater.

They chattered aimlessly as they walked down the long, dipping hill to the next village. At first, there was only the bubble of summer birdsong, the occasional rasp of a motorcycle on the faraway bypass. Then, as they neared the village, they heard the sharp thump of music on the evening air and they thrilled with anticipation.

"The thing about dos like this," said Alison with an air of experience that was utterly unjustified, "is that you never know how they're going to turn out."

78

She was to remember the remark later.

As the two girls approached the Village Hall, Alec Lucas
was approaching Sue's flat. It was at the top of a brand-new,
dressed-stone hall of residence that stood in a leafy campus
in one of the city's closer suburbs. It was an area of avenues
and groves, detached villas and municipal flowerbeds.
Because of the city's road pattern, it was a quiet suburb, a
place that people drove to but never through.

Sue, as well as lecturing and researching at the
University, had taken on the duties of resident warden for
the hall of residence. The flat went with the duties.

"Why not?" she'd asked Alec on their first meeting in the
library. "It's a super flat and I get a beautifully subsidised
rent. Costs me peanuts. And apart from summer courses for
the O.U., the whole damn building's mine every vac."

Dad parked his car in front of the building and noticed
the usual collection of academic transport: estate cars,
vintage tourers, sensible economy models and one van. He
crossed a little bridge over an artificially re-routed stream,
entered the shiny-floored reception area and headed for the
lifts. The hall porter looked up from a portable television set
and nodded. Dad entered the lift, which had carpets on its
walls and a rosy mirror on its back. He pressed the button
for the top floor.

Sue was, he estimated, in her early thirties. She was tall
and healthy, with red hair. She dressed well, spoke well and
was obviously very bright. Her ex-husband had travelled a
great deal and had finally lost patience with returning to a
home filled with Sue's academic friends. They had parted
amicably. She had told him all this and more at their first
meeting. She talked a lot and touched people a lot. She
wasn't in the least like Helen. That didn't stop Alison's Dad
from finding her disturbingly attractive. He realised that Sue
was the first single woman he'd talked to at any length since
Helen had gone. He would have to be careful. She admired
the school books he wrote for a living and said so. Flattery

was dangerous.

The lift doors opened on to a thickly carpeted hallway. Various doors that looked like maintenance access opened off one side of the hall. On the other, facing him, was the door to Sue's flat. He could hear soft music. Vivaldi. What else?

It wasn't that he didn't like parties. He didn't like himself at parties. When he watched the crazed cheerfulness of other people as they drank, danced, ate, chattered, he turned numb. Ideas dried up, conversation limped, he heard himself and he winced. He thought of Alison in the Village Hall and felt envious. At her age, parties were uncomplicated fun.

Sue opened the door and smiled at him.

"You made it. Good."

"Did you think I wouldn't?"

"Wasn't hundred per cent certain. After all, I did rather pick you up, you had a hunted look."

"Terrible places, these libraries. Moral minefields."

"Come in and meet people."

It was a spacious, modern flat, smart with light grey and red furnishings, uncluttered and tidy. The music came from an expensive looking tower of silver and black boxes with big, free-standing speakers. There were a lot of books. A round table was covered with nibbles, dips and nuts. Ten or twelve people stood or sat about, sipping wine, eating from paper plates and murmuring together. Sue began to steer him round, telling him names that he instantly forgot. He smiled, shook hands and tried to look enigmatic. They all seemed to be University staff or postgraduate students. He was a simple writer of schoolbooks. Mind you, not a bad gardener or local historian by now, either . . .

Sue took him to the kitchen to get a drink. She was not wearing many clothes, he realised, or rather, the clothes she wore did not cover much of her. There was a lot of shoulder showing on one side, acres of shapely back, a slit skirt that peeped out glimpses of a long leg, bare arms and, good Lord, a gap that showed her navel.

80

"What would you like to drink?" she asked when they were alone in the kitchen.

He looked round and saw bottles of white and red wine. He also noticed that they were standing, with careless rapture, bang next to a stack of Sue's autumn lecture notes, which, he assumed, she was working upon. He'd obviously hesitated too long. She opened a wall cupboard, produced a bottle of whisky, raised an eyebrow, received a nod and poured him a drink. She glanced at the lecture notes, then back to Alec.

"You don't think I'm a Serious Academic Person at all, do you?"

"I . . ."

"Well I am. I'm Elected Representative to Convocation now. I may be newsworthy, but I am good, you know. Nice to have you here."

"Why?"

"I know all *that* lot." She gestured towards the living room. "Work with them every damn day, nearly. You're new. That's nice."

Alec said, "Don't get too expectant. I'm probably as boring as anyone else. My daughter says I'm more so."

"How old?"

"Thirteen, nearly fourteen."

"Pretty? Bright? Or both? Like me?"

"Both, I'm afraid."

"Can't be easy for you. That age. Without a Mum."

Alec Lucas looked at this pretty, bright woman and remembered conversations in the night on the balcony.

"How's the haunted house you were telling me about?"

He shrugged. "It's not haunted. Not really. Just . . . Shame it's not, really, I could use a bit of company."

He'd said the wrong thing. Sue was as quick as falling water.

"Then invite me out. I'd love to see it."

"Oh yes, of course." Why had he been brought up to be polite? "You must pop out some time and have a look."

"Good. Sunday? Morning or afternoon?"

He felt waters close over his head. He thought about Alison. Then he heard a whisper in his ears. It was, thank God, Helen, helping him.

"Go on. Invite her. It's high time. It'll do Ally good!"

"Would you," said Alec, "like to come to come to lunch?"

Perhaps because she was so good at lectures, committees and politics, she only had to smile a "Yes". Instead, all she said was "You must draw me a map. I get lost very easily with new friends."

A little later, he was standing in the living room, talking with a big man of about his own age, a history don with a quiet sense of humour which appealed to the Alec Lucas inside Dad. The don looked at Alec's glass.

"Oh-ho. Uisquebaugh, eh? The peaty fluids. Our Susan has admitted you to the inner cupboard. Better lash yourself to the mast and stuff wax in the sailors' lugholes, old boy. I've seen the signs before."

"I'm being chatted up?"

"Fattened up, old boy. Enjoy it. It's very pleasant, until she moves in for the kill. That can be messy. She never seems to mind much, but there are a few bruised male egos standing round this room tonight, you can bet."

"Including . . . ?" Dad moved his glass in his companion's direction. The history don nodded and twinkled.

"I'm not complaining. Every campus should have a Sue. Stops us getting too superior. Good at her job, too. She may move to another place, do a spell across the water, but if you ask me she's got her beadies on the Chair of English here. A.s.a.p. Wants to be a telly-prof. Looking like that, she shouldn't have too much trouble. She's already been on *Any Questions* when it came here, but she's wasted on radio."

Dad glanced across the room. She was looking at him through a group of people deep in a discussion about University politics. She smiled. Lunch on Sunday. Oh Helen. Oh Alison. Oh help.

The music in the Village Hall was as solid as steel. It rattled

82

the metal frame windows, bellied the curtains, chimed the glasses, it even seemed to have power to shift the clouds of cigarette smoke. Alison sat with Edith and Maisie on the edge of a trestle table. Alison and Edith were hand-dancing: Maisie, whose feet didn't quite reach the floor, contented herself with wobbling about in time to the thundering disco. In front of them was a wild and complicated scene, made up of several very different elements.

The older guests, ranging in age from forty to eighty, sat at the rear of the hall, near the kitchens and the trestle tables which served as a bar. The heat was taking its toll. ties were unhitched, the jackets of best suits hung from the backs of metal chairs, and tight shoes were eased off and scuffed under the tables, on each of which stood a lit candle in an empty wine bottle. The tables were the square, folding variety and so unstable that it was common for a bottle to topple and spray candle grease over squealing guests.

Beer and spirits were served by three perspiring young men with bottle openers on strings round their necks and huge, wobbling bellies. From the kitchens flowed a stream of food, both hot and cold. Alison caught glimpses of stout women in pinnies labouring in swirls of steam. She also watched, impressed, as men threaded their way through the thrashing dancers on the floor, nonchalantly carrying six or seven pint glasses at a time without spilling a drop. The dancers, of course, made up another element of the scene, writhing and jumping to the pounding music, through lakes of colour which cascaded down from the disco projector in the rafters. The colours spun, shivered and changed. The dancers were the real birthday guests, in their late teens and early twenties, though Alison had already seen how the nature of the crowd altered with the nature of the music. When the disc jockey calmed the tempo down for a few records, the young people would flock, perspiring, to the bar (men and boys) or to the cloakrooms (girls). Then, parents would sedately quickstep or foxtrot until the young had satisfied all natural functions. The jockey would spot this moment with uncanny accuracy. His blooping microphone would crackle, he would adopt a Deep Southern American drawl, introduce something from the Top Twenty and parents would dive for cover while the floor was given over once again to a heaving, seething tangle of movement.

A group of girls, not much older than Alison, made up a third element of the party. Heavily made-up and painstakingly dressed, they huddled by the stage, rearranging themselves, tossing their heads and, with studied unconcern, trawling for the attention of the boys. Sometimes they were lucky and became a part of the wrestling dance floor or were led outside into the cool darkness. Sometimes they were not. Alison found the whole, wordless ritual ridiculous.

"S'boring," she said, "let's go and *do* something."

"No, I want to hear this one, it's one of my best," said Maisie and stayed, twitching, on the trestle.

"OK," said Edith and followed Alison to the kitchens.

They spent ten minutes putting sausages on trays, sliding them into an oven, taking other trays from another oven and putting the cooked sausages on plates to be passed out to the ever-eating guests.

"If that was boring, this is super-super-boring," said Edith and wandered back into the heaving hall.

Alison got herself an orange squash and stood at the door of the hall, looking in. She was in the building's small reception area, a square of shiny black tiles and noticeboards, with corridors leading off to right and left. To the right, lavatories and committee rooms. To the left, cloakrooms and another committee room. It was a well-used Village Hall.

A door banged to her right and she heard footsteps. They stopped, just behind her.

"Haway," said a voice she knew and she relaxed.

"Haway yourself," she said without turning. Tommy Saddler was pleased about this. It gave him time to finish zipping up his jeans.

"What's it like in there?" he asked.

"Noisy."

"Aye. Fine for them as likes it, like. They'll be bashing

away for ages. Midnight, they'll be singing-drunk up the bank and through the village."

There was a pause. Alison considered slipping away and going home to the telly, Cubby and Max. The evening was a disappointment and there was no real reason to continue it. Then Tommy spoke.

"Hey, Alison. D'you want to see a picket line?"

"What?"

"My uncle's outside in the van. We're going over to Ettingham Colliery. Pick up my Dad, his picket-shift's nearly over. Want to come for the ride?"

"Can't. Got to go home soon. Dad won't know where I am."

"Ettingham's only five minutes away. We'll be back in quarter of an hour. We'll drop you at the Coal House. It'd take you longer to walk home."

That was true.

"What's so special about a picket line?"

"Just that I bet you've never seen one."

Alison got her bomber jacket and followed Tommy out to a battered pick-up truck, where a quiet, big man chewed on a pipe and kept the engine idling.

"You took your time, bonny lad."

"Met Alison. She's coming for the ride."

The man grunted as if the news made no difference to him, put the van in gear, and they grated away from the Village Hall.

Alison had hardly spared a thought for the miners' strike for months, which made her realise how long it had been going on. It was on the news every night, but she no longer took it in. Dad had grumbled about coal shortages for the fire, but they seemed to have survived, only lighting a fire now and then and only for its comfort, not its warmth.

It was blessedly peaceful in the cab of the van after the party. Neither Tommy nor his uncle spoke and the van's engine settled to an asthmatic chunter. They headed out of the lower village, east towards the coast, which was a tortuous ten miles away, but they took a road that Dad and she had never tried. It snaked up the side of one of the scarps, through copses of trees and out across sheep fields. It was a hot night, still and close. Alison tensed as a rabbit froze in the headlights, then scuttered frantically away in front of them, weaving from side to side of the lane, looking for escape. Tommy's uncle did not vary his speed. Tommy said "Don't worry, we won't run over him, like."

"Why not? I thought you killed every bunny you saw."

"If we ran over him, right, his skin'd be nae use."

They fell silent again. The rabbit dived into a hedge.

As they crested the top of the scarp, the landscape changed as if someone had switched channels on a television set. Ahead and below them was a moonscape of tips and heaps, a clutter of sheds and huts, a forest of stark pylons and winding gear. Lights were strung from poles, wires criss-crossed the scene, sagging in the heat. The pit village lay on the far side of the workings, huddling away down a slope and reappearing on a far bank.

As the van drew nearer to the mine, Alison saw a chain-link perimeter fence and, a few hundred metres ahead, the concrete service road that led inwards to the pit entrance. Parked in the service road was a high-sided white van with the letters NTV clearly visible. Tommy's uncle swore softly. Alison glanced at him and saw that he was looking beyond the television van to a layby opposite the mine entrance. It was filled with police minibuses.

"The buggers," said Tommy.

"What's wrong?" asked Alison.

"I'll tell y'what's wrong, bonny lass," grunted Tommy's uncle. "We got trouble. Bloody trouble."

Dad became aware that about half of the guests had now left the flat. He had been deep in amusing chat with the likeable history don, talking about nothing in particular but enjoying it. From time to time Sue had come up to them, seen to their needs, smiled, particularly at Dad, and wafted on to another group. Dad checked his watch. Half past ten. He

86

had asked Alison be home at half past ten. He explained to the don and said goodnight. Then he looked around for Sue.

"She's in the kitchen," called a bearded man who was watching television in the corner, with the sound turned right down. On the screen were rows of policemen with helmets and riot shields.

"That's Ettingham," said the bearded man. "Getting close to home, that is."

As if to confirm this, a caption appeared on the screen: ETTINGHAM COLLIERY . . . LIVE.

"Any trouble?" asked Dad, more to be polite than because he had much real interest.

"Not yet. Looks ugly, though."

Again, the cameras proved him right. The picture changed with a swivel and steadied on a line of miners standing in front of the tall gates. They were waving their arms and shouting. One pushed to the front and bowled a brick forwards. The hand-held camera wobbled and ducked, following the brick. It hit a police riot shield and bounced away. The roadway was littered with stones and glass.

"Nasty," said Dad and went into the kitchen, where he found Sue kneeling on a stool and rummaging in a top cupboard. She was showing a lot of herself. She looked down at him. That smile again.

"Don't tell me. You've got to go."

"Alison. She'll be getting home now."

"Has she got a key?"

"Oh yes, but . . ."

"Well then. Stay a bit longer."

"No, really. I can't."

"I know. Teasing. Don't want to lose you yet, Alec."

She got down and stood very close to him. He felt rather than saw her gently push the kitchen door closed.

"Until Sunday lunch, then? What time shall I arrive?"

"Twelve? We'll have a snifter in the village pub first. It's nice. They let kids in, too."

87

"How nice of you to call me a kid, Alec."

"I meant . . ."

"I know what you meant. Silly."

Then she was kissing him. She was very good at kissing.

As he drove home through the lanes beyond the city he thought about four things. He thought that his daughter would be home by now and would rib him for staying out late. He thought that he had probably taken a whisky too many in order to stay a little longer at a party that he had, unexpectedly, enjoyed. He thought that he hadn't been kissed like that for a long time. And he thought that he also couldn't remember when anyone had called him by his Christian name instead of Mister Lucas or Dad.

When he got home, Alison was not there.

A policeman waved them down at the entrance to the service road, near the television van. He walked towards them, black in the headlights. Tommy's uncle swore again and stopped the van.

"Why don't y'put your foot down and go through?" asked Tommy.

"Aye, and how far would I get through a hundred coppers? And what about you two?"

Tommy glanced at Alison and nodded. It was as if she got in the way of a masculine venture. She felt a burden. Then the policeman was at the window, talking.

"Excuse me, can you tell me your destination, sir?"

The voice that came from Tommy's uncle shocked Alison. Gone were the silences and grunts. His words came in a tight, spitting snarl.

"If you mean where I'm gannin', I'm gannin' to join the pickets and relieve me brother. So if you don't want any of your lot under me wheels, tell 'em to move. We're lawful pickets."

"I'm sorry, sir, but our orders are quite clear . . ."

"Shove yer orders!"

". . . and we have reason to expect that some working

miners are about to report for duty. It's our job . . ."

"Shut yer gob, man, you're not from round here, I can tell that. Bugger off home and leave us be."

". . . our job to make sure they can attend their lawful place of work if they so wish."

Tommy suddenly leaned across his uncle: "Y'talk like a bloody telephone book, man. Bugger off."

The policeman abandoned his official air.

"Right, that's it. Out, the lot of you! Sarge! Over here!"

"Ah've got bairns in the van, man! Gan away!"

"Aye, a lassie and all!" shouted Tommy.

"And what the hell's she doing here?" The voice came from beside Alison's window and she jumped in her seat. The police sergeant, wearing an ugly helmet with a visor, was wrenching at the door handle and glaring through the open window at her.

"Gannin' aboot her lawful business, so get yer dirty hands off of me van!" snarled Tommy's uncle.

There were several policemen round the van now and Alison heard one of them say to another: "You wouldn't credit it, would you? Bringing wee girls along for protection."

Alison felt like crying, not from fear but from frustration. She couldn't understand what was behind all the hatred. Why were they so abusive to each other? Why didn't they talk instead of shouting? She was reminded of Tommy and his gang in the playground at school, gangs that fought each other, not for a reason, but because that was what gangs were for. She checked that her door was locked on the inside. Tommy noticed.

"Good lass," he said, "you're one of us now."

"Only if I choose to be," snapped Alison.

Tommy looked at her quizzically, but there was no time for discussion. Alison squealed. The van was being rocked from side to side and a policeman was chanting "Out, out, out" while Tommy's uncle let rip with some of the ripest language Alison had ever heard. She was frightened now. She could imagine the van crashing over. The engine was still running. There might be fire. She had bad dreams about fire.

Suddenly, the rocking stopped. There were shouts and running feet. Alison sat upright in her seat.

Ahead of them, approaching the mine entrance, was a single decker coach. She saw the driver's white face. The coach seemed to be empty.

"The bastards," said Tommy, "they're lying on the floor so's nobody sees 'em."

"Don't worry, we know who they are, lad," said his uncle.

Alison noticed that a ragged crowd of men had collected by the gate, beyond the police cordon. They began to shout as they saw the coach. Suddenly, the air was busy with threats and thrown stones. The police raised tall riot shields to protect themselves. Some of the miners had dustbin lids or squares of plywood. There came a shrill, shouted order and the police ran full tilt at the men by the gate.

"Me Dad's in there!" yelled Tommy, struggling to get out of the van.

"Sit still and keep yer head down!" barked his uncle. "Ye can do nowt out there!"

Alison gazed out, horrified. Beneath the arc lights of the mine gates, men struggled, pushed, kicked, bit, punched and screamed. Police ranks broke, reformed, fell back, reformed again. Men fell to the ground on both sides and were booted indiscriminately. Truncheons flashed. She heard thuds and yells of pain. A hurled brick bounced off the road and clanged on the van's bonnet. She heard a siren and more police arrived, spilling from their vehicles and running as soon as their boots hit the ground. On a grass verge beyond the fighting she caught glimpses of three men who seemed to be dancing a jig. One had a television camera harnessed to his shoulder, one held a sausage-shaped microphone towards the fight, the third was gabbling at a stick in his hand, ducking to avoid missiles.

"Telly newsmen," said Tommy. "They've got enough to film tonight, and all."

Tommy's uncle shook his head sadly. "This has been

90

brewing up long enough. I never thought it would go this far, mind. It's madness, this."

Alison saw a policeman standing on the roof of a Land Rover. He was calling through a loudhailer, trying to calm matters down. She couldn't catch all the words but heard "lawful" and "riotous assembly" and "peaceably disperse before . . ." Whatever the policeman said, it had the opposite effect to his intention: from the miners' ranks, far at the back, a bottle spiralled into the air. It was no ordinary bottle. From its neck fluttered a ribbon of fire. It fell inside the churning mass of police and shattered on the road. Alison saw an instant blossom of flame, bigger, higher and fiercer than she could have imagined. Policemen scattered, yelling warnings. The fuel spread and burned. She saw a policeman running, his back and legs rippling with flames. He fell and rolled over. His colleagues dropped beside him and beat at him to quench the fire before it reached his body.

A flicker in the night sky, a smash and another fire-flower bloomed.

This time it landed harmlessly, but this time it tripped a switch in the police-machine. There were crucial, called orders. The policemen massed, their numbers now trebled by the reinforcements, formed ranks and hurled themselves towards the picket lines with a new purpose. The fight was tight, a close, surging mass of bodies. The shouting died, giving way to a strenuous, breathless muttering of men. Alison and Tommy could hear only the occasional bark or hiss, the thud of a hard object against softer matter, a yelp of pain or triumph. The television crew crept closer to the fight, squinting, pointing, chattering with their equipment. Alison watched them with disgust. She was empty with loathing for everything she'd seen, but most of all she ached with hatred for the trio of men who were sucking up the violence and sending it through their clever equipment to entertain the rest of the world. Quietly, so that neither Tommy nor his uncle could hear, she unlocked her door. Slowly, she eased the handle down. She paused for a moment until she was sure that the boy and the man had

91

noticed nothing.

Then she was out and off, running through the petrol-stinking night air.

Alec Lucas had telephoned Edith's house. No answer. He had phoned Maisie's house. Maisie's Dad had answered: "Haway, they'll be at it a bit yet. Look, I'm going down to pick up our lass in half an hour. I'll collect Alison and drop her off for you, OK?"

He was relieved. The whisky had clouded him more than he thought and he didn't fancy turning out again. He made a coffee and switched on the television. He watched it with half his mind: the other half was wondering what to do about Sue.

After a minute or two he sat up straight and forgot all about Sue. The television was talking about a riot on the picket lines at Ettingham Colliery, just over the hill from the Coal House. The pictures reminded him of the ones he'd seen at Sue's flat, but they were horribly changed. There was raw fighting, flames sprang across the screen, an ambulance blotted out the picture and moved on. There was talk of injury.

And then, running towards the camera, was his daughter. She was yelling, drowning out the reporter's attempts at a commentary:

"Go away! Go on, scram! You're making it worse! You're just – just vultures! Can't you see? These are people's Dads! They're having a bad enough time without you lot snooping and sniffing around! Get out!"

Dad was out of his chair and racing, whisky fumes and kisses forgotten. For the second time that summer, his car tyres smoked and slewed up the drive as he headed for his daughter and her problems.

"That was Sue on the phone. I told her that was you on the telly. She saw you. Says you'll be a national phenomenon.

Appear on chat shows."

"Who?"

They were home. It was midnight and Dad was sitting on the edge of her bed while she sucked at a cup of cocoa.

"You could have been hurt, badly."

"Who's Sue? Don't change the subject."

"Ally, the strike. It's not your fight."

Oh yes it is, she thought. It is now. She remembered how a policeman had bundled her away from the camera crew and into a minibus. How Tommy had come hammering and yelling at the door until he, too, was hauled inside. A policeman had kept an eye on them, but his attention was pulled to the fighting. Walkie talkies squawked, men ran past, orders were bawled, firelight slithered across the condensation on the minibus windows. It was a red, raw, reeking nightmare.

She looked at Tommy, but Tommy was staring at the floor, his knuckles white, his lips moving silently. His Dad. She touched his knee. He shook his head but kept it down.

The back doors of the minibus clicked and opened and there was Dad, peering inside with a lost and frightened look. Behind him was a police officer, cap gone, blood smearing his forehead, anxious to get children and fathers off his hands. Addresses were exchanged, elbows gripped and marching orders given. She tried not to look towards the mine gates as Dad hustled her and Tommy towards his car. It was parked behind the van, which hadn't moved. Tommy's uncle was leaning on the bonnet, head in hands. Dad stopped for a few words, which ended in Tommy getting a clip round the ear from his uncle and a bundle up into the cab. While that was going on, Alison leaned backwards and to one side and saw desolation.

The television crew were loading up and preparing to leave. The picket line was halved in size. The men stood by the gate, huddled and quiet. Out of the gates, driving fast and flanked by police cars, came the single decker coach. It swept past and away. There was a solitary cry of "Scab-helper!" but no throwing or struggling. Instead, a ring of police, two deep, all with helmets, visors and shields, surrounded the gates and the pickets. A few flames still tickled the concrete surface of the road. Two policemen in anoraks were sweeping up litter with wide brooms. The last of several ambulances bumped down off the grass verge and swung away, headed for the city hospital. The night was filled with echoes. Alison and Dad drove home in silence and made cocoa.

"It's my fight as much as anyone's."

"Why?"

"Dad, you should have seen them! They would have done anything to keep the strike going. Anything! Died, even!"

"And that makes it your fight?"

"The police were horrible."

"They weren't. They don't enjoy that sort of thing. They have a job to keep the law in one piece. You don't think they enjoy all that fighting, do you?"

"They looked as if they did."

"And the miners didn't?"

"Look Dad," she said after a pause that lasted long enough for her to admit that some of the miners had been more than enthusiastic in their petrol bombing, how many had cheered hysterically when the policeman caught fire, "Look Dad, you dragged us up here, right, you think this place is so great, right, you can't exactly moan because I'm identifying with local causes, can you?"

Dad sighed and rubbed his eyes.

"Ally, think it through. There are no end of arguments on both sides of the pit strike. Think them through and decide for yourself by all means. But don't suddenly pin your colours to the local flag just because you've decided to settle down. Better to think how you can help the people who are suffering because of the strike. But you must let those who started it, finish it. There is no point in jumping up and down in front of TV cameras and running the risk of being injured. When all's said and done, *neither* of us really could say who's right and who's wrong."

"The miners are right. They want their jobs back.

They're good at their jobs. People won't let them work. And, and . . ."

"Steady on, Ally."

". . . don't you see? There's nothing else for them to do! Dad, those policemen had shields and helmets and sticks. The miners had nothing. It's just not equal."

"I love you. I'm proud of you. I disagree with you. Now, love, go to sleep."

The room went black and Dad moved to the door.

"Wonder how Tommy's Dad is," she said.

"They took him to hospital. He didn't look too bad, though."

"Dad?"

"Yes?"

"Who's Sue? You never said, in the end."

"You'll meet her on Sunday. She's coming to lunch."

"No, I mean is she my age, or one of you lot?"

"Nearer mine than yours. She's the woman who had the party tonight."

"Why's she coming to lunch?"

"Why not?"

She snuggled down and remembered that she hadn't seen Cubby or Max since they'd returned from the riot.

"Where are the cats?"

"In the stable, asleep. Goodnight."

The door closed and she listened to Dad creaking downstairs. Sue. Bloody hell. Trouble there.

The two cats clung together on top of an old wardrobe in the cool stable. Cubby was trembling, Max was watchful. She was staring at the square of light that shone through the hole in the door where they came and went. It was slight, pale moonlight, but the only gleam in the small-hours darkness.

Both cats knew there was something out there. They had seen it. They had run for safety.

Max watched and waited for the square of light to darken,

95

as it would if a black shape fell across it. Cubby fell into a nap, crammed with images of black pillars that moved.

Chapter 8

Geordie Harrison sat by the empty fireplace in the pub and supped his brown ale. He took it slowly, making it last. It was a Thursday afternoon and he didn't collect his pension until Friday mornings.

Geordie looked at, rather than watched, a portable television set that stood on the bar. It was showing black and white pictures of a horse race. Unusually for the village, Geordie was not a racing man. Neither was Harry the landlord, who leaned lugubriously on the bar and half watched the cantering horses on the smoke-stained screen. Harry did not think of himself as a naturally lucky man. More to the point, he had spent the morning drawing up the week's takings to date. The strike was denting his turnover to the point where he would soon have to ask the brewery for help, a step he did not want to take.

"Ye'll have to get this fire lit soon, bonny lad."

"Aye, the year's drawing in, Geordie."

"Not a bad summer."

"It's been canny. Mind, that usually means we're in for some brass monkey weather come winter."

"Why, ye canna tell, man. Billy the postman reckons the moles are digging deep, so it'll be cauld, like, and Mabel at the Post Office says the birds are going away late so it'll be mild. It's all bloody daft, man."

Harry lit a small cigar and a horse won the race on television by a clear length.

"Aye," he said, glancing up as a delivery van reversed into the car park outside the window. "I always listen to the older folk. They generally seem to have a better idea of things like that."

"And there's enough of the owd buggers about to give ye their opinions and all," grumbled Geordie, whose gout was giving him gyp. "Some of them round here don't know when to die off and that's a fact."

"Who's the oldest we got then, Geordie?"

"Why I couldn't rightly say. Might be Old Man Saddler, Ted's Dad. Or Mabel's Mam, she's a canny age. Or it might even be Old Shotton, the old Pit Foreman's son."

"Who's he?"

"Ah, ye probably wouldn't know him, Harry. Keeps to himself. Have to be up very early or very late to catch Old Shotton. Lives alone and lives clean. Must be well in his eighties, that one. Queer bugger. Strange life. They say . . ."

A young man came in, delivering crisps and peanuts. Harry signed a receipt, the young man left and the early afternoon hush fell on the bar again. Geordie forgot what he was going to say.

"Haven't seen much of that chap Lucas from the Coal House lately," said Harry, relighting his cigar. "Seems to work a lot."

"Canny lass of his, that Alison."

"Aye. Thirteen, eh? See her on the telly the night they had that do at Ettingham?"

"Naw, I was in here, man. Heard about it."

"I reckon her Dad might be courting again. Seen this piece from the city, keeps coming out, drives a sports car. Big girl, mind, very leggy." Harry made a certain gesture.

"Dinna tempt me, Harold, I'm ower old to think of that."

"Could do with a woman over there, though. What the bairn would make of it I couldn't say."

"Go on, I'll have another bottle of brown."

That first Sunday lunch had set the tone right from the

98

start.

Dad had fussed in the kitchen all morning, listening to the radio and roasting a leg of lamb with garlic and rosemary. Alison didn't like garlic and Dad knew it, but he used it all the same. She had to lay the table and uncork bottles of wine and polish the wine glasses and toss a salad in French dressing which Dad knew she didn't like either. At least she preferred it to the chilled beetroot soup which was waiting in the fridge "because it's easier at the last minute" whatever he meant by that.

Towards noon Dad disappeared upstairs and came down without his pinny, wearing a new sweater and looking falsely unconcerned. He poured himself a whisky and stood by the french windows, humming nervously.

Alison went out into the garden and distanced herself from the house. Cubby and Max were racing up and down a willow tree, striking impossible poses on the slightest of twigs. She watched them for a while and then wandered down through the trees. On the far side of the wood was a slight bank overlooking the road that ran up the hill and into the village. She stood on the bank, watching the world. It was mild, overcast, still. Up at the top of the hill the pub was opening and she saw the little knot of regulars disperse from their waiting place by the bus stop and burrow through the open door. One of them, Mabel the postmistress, was late. Alison smiled as she watched the dumpy figure scurry out of the village and almost run into the pub for her stout and crisps.

She heard a car coming up the hill, a sporty, racy noise. It was a little red open-top car, shining and new. As it approached the circle of sycamores, it slowed, then stopped with its engine running, just below and slightly to the left of Alison who looked down on its driver. She was a tall, pretty woman with a cloud of red hair held in a white silk scarf. She wore a white boiler suit over a bright green shirt. Red and green, thought Alison, should never be seen. The woman in the car was feeling in the glove compartment. She drew out a piece of paper with a hand-drawn map on it which she inspected before looking around her.

"God, it's her. She's the one who's coming to lunch. Gordon Bennett, she's a bit young for Dad!"

Alison wondered if she should show herself and direct this Sue-woman to the Coal House, but she didn't wonder long. Let her find her own way. Got a map, hadn't she? Dad probably drew it for her so she wouldn't get lost. Poor little thing. Big thing.

The Sue-woman put the car into gear and drove on up the hill. As Alison turned back into the trees she saw a twinkle of red as the car slowed and bumped into their drive. Oh well. Cubby and Max crouched and watched her as she walked slowly under the willow tree and headed for the house.

The white boiler suit was already in the living room, enthusing about the house to Dad when Alison entered and stood in the doorway.

"It's wonderful! Amazing! Not a bit what I expected. Heavens, you'd never know it was here unless you knew it was here!"

Alison thought this an idiot thing to say and suppressed the knowledge that she'd said almost exactly the same thing to Maisie and Edith earlier in the year.

"And this is Alison. Hi!"

"Hello."

"Love your jacket!"

"Oh Ally, you're not wearing that old thing again, are you?"

"Looks like it, Dad. Doesn't it."

Dad shied away from confrontation. He turned to the Sue-woman. "Drink?"

"You promised we'd all go to your nice pub. The one where they let children in."

Alison resented this bitterly even though she could see it was some kind of shared joke. Some joke. They went to the pub.

The pub was Sunday-lunchtime-bustly, smoky and companionable. The three of them sat at a corner table.

100

Dad had a pint of beer, the Sue-woman had a gin and Martini and Alison had a coke. She watched how the men in the bar eyed up the white boiler suit, casually, so that they wouldn't be spotted by their mates or wives. Old Geordie Harrison winked and waved at Alison.

"Hello, bonny lass, gannin' canny?"

But even he was getting an eyeful of the Sue-woman. Alison furiously confessed to herself that the red hair and green shirt looked stunning together, after all. The Sue-woman had green eyes, which helped, but were an unfair advantage. Alison suddenly noticed Tommy Saddler's father. He was reading the Leek Club notices which were pinned up beside the dart board. There was a sticking plaster on his forehead and one hand was bandaged. The other held a pint.

"Excuse me a mo," said Alison and went over to the noticeboard.

"Quite the local lass. Who's she speaking to?"

"Not sure. Might be one of her friends' fathers."

Ted Saddler started when the girl touched his arm, spilling some beer on his boots.

"Sorry."

"Ah, that's all right. Alison, is it? From the Coal House?"

"Yes." She saw him searching her face for signs of airgun pellet scars. She smiled.

"Don't worry. Gone now. I came to see how you were. I heard they took you to hospital. On Friday night. I was there."

"Aye, I heard. Our Tom's a daft little sod, bringing a lassie to a do like that. He won't do it again in a hurry, I can tell you."

"Wasn't his fault. He wasn't to know. And anyway, it was up to me whether I went or not. How are you, Mister Saddler?"

Ted wasn't used to being called Mister and savoured it for a moment.

"Nae so bad. They didn't keep me in, like. Bust a bone in the hand, got a few cuts and bruises. I'll do."

"It was horrible. I'm on your side."

"My side?"

"The miners. I'll do anything to help if I can."

"Oh aye? And what are you going to do, bonny lass? Run a soup kitchen at the big house?"

There was an ugly note to the man's voice which he obviously recognised himself. He patted her shoulder with his bandaged hand.

"Na, that wasn't meant like that. Best thing you can do is steer clear of picket lines, girl. It gets nasty sometimes. We're ready for it, you're not. But thanks for asking after me, anyway."

She got the impression he was feeling awkward in front of his mates, talking to a young girl about the strike. She gave him a small smile and went back to the corner table.

"What was all that about, love?"

"Oh," said Alison airily, "just pledging solidarity with the miners. Discussing tactics."

"Give me strength."

"No, give me another dry Martini instead," said the white boiler suit with an amused expression.

While Dad was at the bar, the woman leaned towards the girl. Here we go, thought Alison, all girls together, let's get to know one another, I'm sure we'll be the best of friends.

"You don't like me much, do you?"

Alison flushed and blustered. She hadn't been ready for that.

"Hardly know you."

"Doesn't matter, one can usually tell straight off. But really, I'm pretty harmless. Probably no more than a ship that passes. No danger."

"We don't usually get many visitors."

"Exactly. Probably do your old Dad a spot of good."

"He's not that old!"

"Precisely."

Alison wondered what she meant but Dad came back with the drinks before she could work it out.

Later, they walked back to the house, had chilled soup

and lashings of roast lamb. Sue insisted Alison have a glass of wine which Alison forced down, not because she liked the dry, metallic taste, but because she was determined to narrow the age gap around the table. She was not going to be the child. She was going to be wary. This woman was clever and that usually meant dangerous. The conversation was about university life, Dad's books, Alison's school and, inevitably, the Coal House. Alison told her about the death of the little girl in the photograph. After lunch Dad lit a cosmetic fire and Alison showed Sue the box of maps and cuttings from Tommy's grandad. Sue seemed interested, though Alison couldn't be certain how genuine the interest was: perhaps she was being humoured. It was hard to tell with Sue.

The woman stayed right through the afternoon. She and Dad played records and talked. Alison was appalled at the records Dad put on. Favourites from his youth, probably, but tunes Alison vaguely remembered from her earliest days, when Dad and Mum would play them and Alison would listen from her bedroom. As far as she knew, Dad had never played them since.

Alison spent large chunks of the afternoon in her room with Cubby and Max. Sue stayed on for a bread and cheese supper, then they all watched a comedy programme on television. Alison kept her eye on the clock, watching bedtime creep nearer. Were they waiting for her to go to bed so that they could be alone? She'd hang on to the bitter end, just see if she wouldn't. She felt guilty when that proved unnecessary.

"Well, must be off," said Sue suddenly, stretching like a cat. "Papers to mark tomorrow, term in less than a week."

"I'll see you out," said Dad, slipping on the casual shoes he'd earlier slipped off when he and Sue were curled up on the big sofa.

"It's been a smashing day. Really." Sue smiled at Alison and Alison knew that this time she meant what she said.

"I'd love to come again. If you'll put up with me."

Alison mumbled something and then they were at the

front door. To her surprise, Sue kissed her warmly on the cheek and winked at her. Then Sue kissed Dad in the same way. She didn't wink at Dad, but she squeezed his hand and looked right into his eyes for a long moment.

The little red car twinkled away into the night, which was keen with the first frosts of autumn. Autumn came early up here, thought Alison. The summer is too short.

They cleared up together, not talking much. On the way to bed Dad paused to rake out the fire. Alison hesitated.

"Well," said Dad from his crouching position at the hearth, "that wasn't so bad, was it?"

"All right."

"What do you think of her?"

"What do *you* think of her, more like."

"She's a friend. She's fun. That's all."

"All right then. Just as long . . ." and Alison went to bed.

Dad stayed by the dying fire a little longer. Helen didn't come. He went to bed feeling guilty. He also felt angry with himself for feeling guilty. He slept badly.

As Harry the landlord had noticed, the autumn brought more and more frequent visits of Sue to the Coal House. On two occasions, she stayed the whole weekend, arriving on Friday evening and leaving early on Monday morning. She slept in one of the spare rooms. Alison kept her eye on this arrangement, but it seemed watertight.

Opinions about Sue's increasing presence varied throughout the village. Geordie Harrison, as easy going as ever, admired the whole arrangement. Billy the milkman, asked to leave extra bottles, drew his own conclusions and spread them liberally. Maisie was thrilled at the hint of romance and quizzed Alison endlessly. Edith stoically affirmed that "it was bound to happen sooner or later, men are like that, even Dads." Tommy Saddler, who still helped out in the garden and still added to his stock of rabbit skins, found the tall woman's presence disturbing. He had worked his way into a more or less easy familiarity with Alison and her Dad.

The newcomer brought a breath of the city and of alien, university ways. She was always well dressed, while Alison's Dad became more and more rustic, increasingly familiar as one of the villagers, even though he lived in the big house. Peter Robson was respectful, but felt that the new lady showed an interest in his garden work which was superficially enthusiastic but forced. Peter was bringing on some prize leeks for the coming Show which were, even in his book, outstanding. The new lady admired them but did not seem to realise that she was looking at potential champions. Strange.

Alison kept her thoughts to herself. Towards Sue herself, she mellowed a great deal. Sue was good company, funny and often outrageous. She had the knack of seeing the world, if not from Alison's standpoint, from Alison's side of the fence. She talked to Alison as an equal and gave no quarter to their age difference. Alison approved of her clothes and make-up, areas in which Sue was forthcoming with valuable tips and advice.

At the same time, it was obvious that the link between Sue and Dad was growing stronger. Sue was out to get him. Liberties were taken, routines were established, at any point where familiarity could be encouraged, Sue encouraged it. Alison began to realise that it was entirely possible that Sue could become her new mother. She didn't know what to think about the prospect. She only had and could only ever have one, dead Mum. Could she have Sue as a friend? It seemed so. Did she want Sue as a friend? She didn't know. Did Dad want Sue as a wife? She couldn't tell. When she tried to nudge Dad towards expressing an opinion, he wandered off in another direction.

"You like Sue, don't you."

"Um. Yes. Don't you?"

"Quite. How much do you like her? I mean, really like her?"

"Quite a lot, I suppose."

"I mean, are we going to go on seeing her every weekend and that?"

"Up to her, I suppose. Why?"

"I mean, she might just as well live here, the amount of time she spends."

"Oh, hardly. Besides . . ."

"Besides what?"

"Um. She's got a place of her own. Have you done your homework yet?"

Often, usually in bed, Alison asked her Mum for help. It didn't come. This was not the sort of situation they had ever shared, so echoes of advice were absent. Alison would lie in the soft darkness, hearing the tumult of air in the leaf-shedding trees and see that this was one problem she would have to cope with alone. There were others. Dad seemed troubled, distant. She thought he was drinking too much.

Dad thought so, too.

On a wild evening when the gales were thrashing the last of the sycamore leaves from the woods, he stood with his whisky on the balcony again. By now, he had taken to keeping an old donkey jacket in the bedroom: the night air on the balcony was salty and sliced with North-Easterly winds. Still, he kept to his routine of a nightcap on the balcony. As long as the gales stayed in the North-East quarter, they were pushed away by the side of the house, leaving a cold but still oasis outside his bedroom. The nightcap, however, had often become two or even three. The donkey jacket was not the only comfort he had taken to keeping in the bedroom.

Work was sticky. The University pestered him for reports. He had finished one textbook and sent it to London, where it received, at best, muted praise. Now he was working on the second, on "Understanding Poetry". It was murderously slow going. His desk was an oil rig of reference books, overshadowing his tired typewriter. The bank had written him a severe letter. The car needed a service. Peter Robson's gardening hours were creeping up as the day of the village Leek Show crept nearer. He had ordered more coal and anthracite for the winter and shuddered at the expense. Alison had brought home a school letter about a

106

January skiing trip and pleaded with him to be allowed to go: the list of 'necessary equipment' had almost caused a seizure.

Helen wasn't there any more. He tried to talk to her but found that he was constructing both sides of the conversation instead of hearing her calm wisdom inside his head. He could picture her, as he would picture her until he died. He could imagine what she would say about the situation. But she no longer spoke out of the night.

He looked into his second whisky.

Sue. Alison. Sue. Alison.

He knew what Sue wanted now. It wasn't what his daughter suspected. Sue did not see herself as mistress of a straggling pile in a reclaimed coalfield. She enjoyed her visits to the Coal House, but only because she enjoyed his company and, yes, Alison's. Sue wanted to marry him. She wanted them to buy a stylish, detached house in an academic suburb of the city: she even had her eye on one, the property of a colleague who had given her first refusal. She wanted them to become a delightful and delicious family of three, a minor jewel in the university's social treasury. A ready-made family, needless to say, for Sue abhorred the idea of pregnancy and labour, let alone nappies. Sue's vision was of a swift and singleminded move from their separate lives to one, corporate life that would be both pleasant and politically successful. (There was no denying, and Sue made no secret of the fact, that she would stand a better chance of becoming Professor of English Literature as a stable, family woman with the right address in the university city.)

Dad sipped his whisky. Which only left his feeling for Sue.

Love was not a word Dad used any more. He did not expect to ever use it again. When he was younger and had first met Helen, the word was rarely off his lips. "I love you", "Much love", "All my love" had been the punctuation marks of their lives. Because it was a tough concept to analyse, he hadn't tried too hard. He knew only that when

107

he held Helen's hand on their first date, there had been a tug of war deep inside him: pulling one way was a deep peace and happiness: tugging the other was a heady swirl of excitement, a need to do and act and be admired. All the time, watching the tug of war was a man with his name who could hardly believe that a girl so good could find good in him, too.

He supposed that was as close to defining love as he would ever come.

He could not say that he loved Sue. He liked her enormously and he found her disturbingly attractive. She was rich company and she had the trick of making him feel less alone than he had felt since Helen had gone. Alison and he shared a third of their lives together as equals. Both Alison and he needed the other two thirds for themselves. That was fair and expected. Sue had taken up a proportion of that emptiness for him. Could she for Alison?

His glass was nearly empty. The night was filled with wind. He stared out into the darkness beneath the trees and let his mind freewheel.

Something moved.

In the black shadow of the tall trees was a blacker shape. It was moving, slowly, following the old drive through the woods. When the gale gusted, the shape swirled. There was someone out there, prowling.

Later, Dad considered if the whisky had given him uncharacteristic bravado. He knew that was not the case. He had become stuck in his thoughts about his life: action, any action, was preferable to more thought.

Behind him, the bedroom curtains shut out all light. If he was careful, he could remain invisible from the woods. He moved across the balcony to the right, putting its width and pillars between him and the shape. He placed his glass on the floor and swung a leg over the railing. His heart raced. He was too old for this sort of thing. Never mind. Onwards, or rather, downwards. He hung from the balcony floor by his fingers, his nose almost touching one of the pillars. This left a drop of about three metres from his trainers to the lawn. He breathed in, straightened himself and let go.

It would have been a perfect landing if his left foot had not come down on the stone base of the pillar. It threw him off balance and he felt a needle of fire scamper up his leg. No point in stopping now. He turned and headed quietly towards the trees. He realised that his stealth was unnecessary. The wind was roaring so loudly in the treetops that he would not have been heard by someone standing beside him. Even the crackling leaves underfoot were swamped by the gale, which tore at his hair and wrenched his jacket. His foot was swelling and shrinking in his shoe but was not, so far, hurting. He concentrated on not being seen.

From the balcony, the black shape had been over to his left, at an angle of forty-five degrees. He estimated it should now be dead ahead, so he struck off slightly to his right, wanting to intercept it. Luckily, this gave him the added cover of a big, old holly thicket and some brambles. He limped round the back of them and approached the point where the old driveway left the trees and headed out into the main lawn. He paused. Unless he had been seen, the prowler should emerge at any moment.

Suddenly, he was scared. It had been difficult to judge from the balcony, looking downwards through trees, but the shape had seemed big. If it came to a fight, he stood no chance. Two whiskies, a sprained ankle and a lifetime sitting on his backside didn't make him much of a favourite in a set-to. He glanced quickly back to the telephone-harbouring house. Too far. Alison's bedroom light was off. Just get on with it. Nothing else to do now.

It was there, in front of him, some five metres away, pacing out from the trees and on to the lawn.

God, it was big. Broad, tall. Broader, from an ankle-length black coat, taller, from a wide-brimmed black hat. Now. It had to be now.

"Hey! You! Stop!"

The huge figure rounded on him, coming to an abrupt halt. He heard a noise that was between a gasp and a whimper, that ended on a rising, querulous note. The figure stood absolutely still, facing him.

It was as if he faced a monolith carved from jet. The hat's brim hid the face in deep shadow, the armless cloak rippled in the wind but revealed nothing. There was a frightening stillness about the figure which came from within. It simply stood and faced him, waiting. Dad swallowed hard.

"Who are you? What do you want?" Silence. "What are you doing here?"

Silence. Just the wind and the thick flapping of the black cloak.

"Look, it's late at night and you're trespassing. What do you want here?"

Silence. Wind.

Then, a voice came out of the blackness. It was a man's voice, but it was unexpectedly high and piping. There was a grating, unused quality to it.

It said. "Shtnnnn."

"What?"

"Shtnnnn. Sree. Do narm. Do narm."

"Who are you?"

A note of pleading: "Shtnnnn. My nem Shtnnnn."

"Shotton?"

"Mm. Mm."

Dad walked carefully forward, until he stood right in front of the black, rippling figure. It was then that he realised the figure was not, after all, motionless beneath its cape and flapping hat. Whoever was inside was shaking with a fever of fright. Do narm. Do no harm. Sree. Sorry. Dad began to relax.

"But . . . what are you doing, man? It's nearly midnight. Why are you here?"

"Ssss . . . ssss . . ."

"What? What are you trying to say? What's wrong with your voice? Are you English?"

"Ssssstr. Mm, mm, my sssstr. Here."

"Your sister isn't here. I'm here. My daughter."

The black figure wriggled inside its cape.

110

"Nnce. Nnce."

"I'm sorry?"

"Nnce here. Sssstr."

"What's the matter? Why do you talk like that? Is there anything I can do?"

There was a long pause, while the wind swooped round them. The black figure raised his head to the sky and Dad heard that whimpering sound again. Then, as if he had reached a decision through pain, the figure produced a black-clad arm from beneath the cloak, raised it slowly and, after another hesitation, removed the wide-brimmed hat.

Dad understood why the figure had difficulty talking clearly.

It had no mouth.

Chapter 9

The day of the Annual Leek Show took Dad by surprise. The same was not true of Peter Robson, who, like every other local gardener, saw Leek Show day as the turning point of the year.

Peter was mumpy.

The new Coal House owner had started his tenure in a storm of enthusiasm, working side by side with Peter, buying good tools, the best seed and plants, providing sacks of feed as instructed, why, he had even joined the Leek Club, paid his subs and helped Peter create a trench for prize-strain leeks. But since the appearance of the redhead from the city, Peter had found himself more and more alone in the garden. Not that he minded solitude, or so he told himself. It was more a question of disappointment. He'd had high hopes of Mister Lucas, and he felt let down. And then there was the matter of the prize leeks.

By intricate manoeuvres in the spring, Peter had become the owner of a particularly good strain of champion leek pips. He had brought them on in his own, heated greenhouse and then, once sure of Lucas, had donated the plants to the Coal House garden, where the soil was richer than in his own allotment. The trench had been dug and fed, the plants had been coddled into the crumbling earth and feeding spouts had been fashioned from old, plastic pop bottles. The leeks prospered. They were like toddlers' arms, the flags spiralling away in green ribbons, the thick bases pure white for the statutory six inches. Peter knew they faced stiff competition in the village but foresaw a creditable showing and the strong chance of a respectable placing by the judges. Quite apart from the leeks, which every member of the Leek Club was duty bound to exhibit, Peter was entering, on Mister Lucas's behalf, a pair of prize onions, a pair of dressed potatoes and a tray of mixed vegetables. Peter even sold the Leek Club raffle tickets for Mister Lucas: this entailed long, hard evenings in the pub, something the Coal House owner was disinclined to take on.

On the morning of the Show, Alison came across Peter and Tommy, at the leek trench beyond the old greenhouse. They were carefully rolling back an elaborate canopy of polythene sheeting, and clearing handfuls of straw from around the bases of the massive plants. She watched for a few minutes. It was like watching priests preparing a sacrament.

"What are you doing?"

Tommy looked up: "Getting ready to table the leeks, bonny lass."

"Don't you bonny lass me, we're the same age. Can I help?"

Tommy looked at Peter, who grunted assent. He was still mumpy.

The Show was held in a wooden shed behind the pub. Alison had never seen anything like it. Trestle tables were loaded with vegetables so big and so perfect, she had to touch them to be sure they weren't plastic. A central table was a forest of vases, from each of which cascaded sprays of cut flowers, pom-poms of brightly coloured blossom that made the air heavy with scent. With many other people from the village, she wandered round the exhibits, having a sneaky preview. She saw Maisie and Edith who came over to see her Dad's entries. They lay in their alloted places, each with a neatly written card: *A. Lucas, C. House.*

"Not bad," said Maisie. "For a beginner, like."

"Shouldn't be Dad's name on them. Ought to be Peter's, he did all the work. Well, him and Tommy."

"Your Dad's garden. Your Dad's plants, 'cepting the leeks," grunted Tommy behind them. His voice was breaking. At last.

"Even so, it doesn't seem fair."

"Where is your Dad? He coming?"

"He's back at the house. In one of his moods. He's been a bit funny since the night he sprained his ankle, don't know why."

"Ee, how'd he do that?"

"Says he went for a walk in the trees at night and twisted it. But I found a booze glass on the balcony, I reckon he was, you know, a bit."

Surprisingly, it was Edith who expressed an opinion: "He's probably a soul in torment, like."

"Who? My Dad!"

"His heart," said Edith mysteriously, "is rent. See, he's enjoying the attention of a beautiful temptress but he feels his allegiance is to you and the memory of your Mam, sort of thing."

The three of them gazed at Edith, who blushed.

"What you been watching?" asked Maisie.

"Aye, farm kids always go that way in the end. It's all them cows," said Tommy.

Edith, who stood a good head taller than Tommy, clipped his ear with her gloves. Then the Show Judges arrived and the public was shooed out while deliberations took place behind locked doors.

The girls walked over the fields to Edith's farm for lack of anything better to do. By unspoken agreement, Tommy peeled away and headed back into the village, looking for mischief.

As she walked down the footpath to the farm, Alison found herself thinking of the splendours of the Leek Show. The vegetables, fruit and flowers made a southern Harvest Festival look like a tatty supermarket. She thought of the rows of mean allotments with their rickety sheds, the grey soil that still sparkled with lumps of coal. How could so much goodness be grown out of such unlikely beginnings?

114

More intriguing still, why? The exhibits in the locked shed had cost lifetimes of care, experience, time and money. It would be cheaper to buy them in the shops. She said as much to the others who looked at her across a great divide.

"Silly cow," said Maisie in a friendly manner and they went into a barn to see a litter of kittens.

Up the hill in the Coal House, the telephone rang. Dad, in the study, swore, reached for his walking stick and dot-and-carried into the hall. It wouldn't be the first time the phone stopped before he reached it. It didn't. It was Sue.

"How's the cripple?"

Dad winced. "It's mending. Swelling's going down."

"You're still not going to tell us how you did it, are you."

"I told you. Tripped in the woods."

"You were funny. On the telephone, the day after. Didn't sound like you at all. What's wrong?"

Dad paused before replying. He was remembering a halting, difficult conversation between himself and a deeply scarred man. They had sat in the kitchen drinking coffee late at night. Shotton would go no further into the house. Dad was glad, in case Alison woke up and came downstairs. He was still having trouble with himself, looking at Shotton's face with equanimity.

"Nothing, really. Just a lot on my mind. Work. Deadlines, you know."

"Me?"

"Oh yes, you too."

"Ah well," said Sue's voice with injected breeze, "how about lunch? Three Tuns? La Cupola? My place?"

Dad looked up, through the hall window. He could see the cars clustered round the shed behind the pub.

"I can't, Sue. It's Leek Show day."

He had hesitated too long. Her voice was cool.

"My God, you really have gone native, haven't you. It'll be bloody pigeons and whippets next."

"You could come out and see how I do."

"Alec, object of my desire, if you think I'm putting on green wellies and swanning round a load of greengrocery

115

pretending that a prize leek is the highest flowering of the human endeavour, bog off."

"Tomorrow?"

"Maybe."

Click. Hum.

He sat in the hall for some time. He was listless, tired. He couldn't care less about the Leek Show, but knew he ought to attend. He couldn't be bothered. Sue niggled at him, wanting something he did not have for her. Boundaries, bills and demands were tightening around him. The empty house seemed, for the first time, oppressive, creakily silent and disapproving of him. He longed for Alison to come bawling into the house, flinging noise and nagging all around her, but he had seen her go down the fields with her friends.

One of the cats rubbed his leg and rolled on her back. He tickled the buttons on her tummy without looking to see if she was Cubby or Max. The cat, blissful, purred. It had known no other home, no previous life. It was lucky.

He saw Shotton's wrecked face again and considered what a strange hour they had spent in the kitchen. The big man had not wanted to come into the house at all. They had been about to part when Dad had put some weight on his left foot, hissed with pain and nearly fallen. Instantly, a powerful arm was around him, supporting him under his armpit. The strength was like steel.

"Sorry, Mister Shotton. Twisted it. I'll be OK."

"Nnn. Hsss. Ah hulp'y."

Up through the garden, through the wind and leaves, across the courtyard to the kitchen door, where Dad balanced on one leg and opened up. He gestured for Shotton to go inside. The big figure shook its head emphatically. Dad started to make the sign of a cup and saucer, then stopped. For Heaven's sake, the man wasn't an idiot and he wasn't deaf. The man was disfigured, not dim.

"Look, Mister Shotton. I'm still not sure why you were in the woods or what all this about your sister is. But you're obviously doing no harm and you've just helped me back. Please come in for a cup of tea, at least."

116

Shotton stepped back and scanned the house, uncertain. He was looking for lights.

"There's only my daughter, she's fast asleep. She won't wake."

Shotton was still reluctant. He looked at Dad for a long moment, made a querulous noise that hid a note of exasperation and pointed to his face beneath the brim of his replaced hat.

"I know," said Dad. "It's a shock when you first see it. It . . . frightened me, you're quite right. But you know that. That's why you walk at night, isn't it? Why you wear that hat and keep your cloak collar up? But I don't mind. Really. Please come in, just into the kitchen if you like, for a few minutes."

The truth was, and Dad knew it, that he wanted the company. Shotton was strange, unlooked-for company. That was what Dad found intriguing. Shotton was a new presence. He played no part in the complications that were growing in and around the Coal House. He came out of the night, from the outside.

Dad hobbled inside and held the door open. Slowly, one step at a time, Shotton came into the kitchen. The black figure stood still and massive in the centre of the floor, waiting. Dad pulled a stool from under the worktop and switched on the light. Shotton's gloved hand flew to his face. Dad turned off the light and switched on a small worktop spot instead, angling it away so that it glowed off into a white corner. They had enough light to see by, but not so much as to make Shotton uneasy. Shotton sat down, keeping his hat on. Dad brewed tea.

"Thnk'y. Kine."

"Thank you, Mister Shotton. You nearly carried me home. I'm grateful. You're a strong man, you know."

"Pt. Wok-n. Chp-n."

"Sorry, couldn't get that one . . ."

Shotton looked around him. Dad kept a shorthand pad and felt-tip pen on the worktop. Alison and he used it for lists and messages. Shotton took it, gestured for permission,

117

got it and, to Dad's astonishment, began to sketch a picture. The felt tip flew and squeaked, making loose, flowing lines. A few details, a scribble of shading and the picturegram was finished. Shotton held it out.

There was a picture of a miner, powerfully built and stripped to the waist, hewing coal at a face. Running on from that was a second picture: the same, big figure, striding out with a walking stick along an empty road that wound away over deserted hills. The third picture showed the same man, wearing Shotton's hat and cloak, chopping logs from a fallen tree. Dad looked up.

"You were a miner. You walk a lot. And you keep fit chopping your own logs."

"Ya, ya."

The drawings were breathtaking. So fast, so explicit. Dad saw what an advantage such a talent must be to Shotton and wondered if it had developed as a result of the man's injuries or had always been there. The kettle boiled, the tea was made and the two men sat facing one another.

"Please. Take off your hat if you wish."

Slowly, Shotton removed his hat. Dad paced himself so that he didn't have to take in all of the sight at once. That way, he let the face grow out of the shadows until he could safely look into it. Shotton, more confident now, stared straight back at him.

His head was almost bald, a massive skull with just a grazing of grey stubble on one side. The left ear was a knob of cartilage, the left eye a slit which sloped steeply from outside top to inside bottom. The complete left side of Shotton's face had been moulded downwards and inwards as if by tremendous heat or pressure. The nose was flat, sloping, the cheekbone splayed out beneath the white, white skin. In the dark woods, Dad had seen no mouth, but it was there, a pathetic gap in the ruined jaw, shoved brutally downwards and to one side. Dad suspected damage inside the mouth and larynx, damage that strained sounds out of the man as if they were grudgingly let loose on the world and only with great effort. As he grew used to what he saw,

118

Dad found himself fascinated by Shotton's right eye. It was unharmed, wide open and filled with life. It regarded him across the room with a bright frankness. Dad felt the big man's entire personality shining from the one, good eye. He liked what he saw.

"How did it happen?"

"Lng tum," said Shotton and wrote 1914 on the pad.

"Ilow old were you?"

Shotton underlined the 14 of 1914.

"God. Was it in the pit?"

Shotton nodded and made some gestures. His gloved hands described a caving-in motion. One fist became himself, crushed by pit props and coal. Then he looked round and pointed to the gas rings beside him.

"Fur."

Buried alive and burned at the age of fourteen.

"Were others hurt, too?"

Shotton held up ten fingers, then three more. He ran a finger across his throat.

"Mm. Ony un ow."

He, the fourteenth, had survived. Lucky fourteen? Unlucky fourteen? Dad watched as Shotton carefully sipped his tea: a lifetime's practice had allowed him to curl the cup under his chin, tilt it and suck from the surface of the liquid. There was an economy in everything he did. Now there was a little light, Dad saw that the old black cloak was shiny with age. He noticed a scrupulously neat darn near the hem and suddenly remembered the scrap of black cassock he'd once seen on the fence in the woods. Cassock was an appropriate thought. There was about the old man a clerical cleanliness only found in certain types of lifelong bachelors. Dad had to assume that Shotton was a bachelor.

"Where do you live, Mister Shotton?" he asked, but Shotton was not keen to be specific. He waved away in the direction of the higher woods behind the village and made a dismissive sign with one hand.

Dad lit a cigarette and offered one to Shotton. The right eye gleamed and wrinkled. The old man took one of the

119

cigarettes, carefully broke off the filter tip and accepted a light. Smoking sideways from his tiny mouth he experienced obvious pleasure. The eye twinkled again.

"Dnn smuk mch. Cnnn frd."

Dad wanted to give him the packet but knew it would be an insulting thing to do.

"Tell me, what's this about your sister? Can you tell me?"

Shotton thought hard. Clearly, it was a complicated message to get out. The old man came to a decision and opened the top of his cloak, startling Dad with a glimpse of very white shirt and pinstripe waistcoat. From an inside pocket, Shotton took an old envelope. He handed it to Dad. Inside was a photograph, a studio portrait taken in sepia and mounted in a stiff card folder. The portrait showed a solemn, slim girl of perhaps twelve or thirteen, wearing a white dress, a ribboned hat and holding a parasol. She sat in front of a painted, sylvan landscape. On the back of the folder was a printed legend, *Marks & Son, Portrait Photography*, and an address in the city. Dad turned back to the photograph and looked at the girl's long, fair hair, the unmistakable look of endurance in the eyes as she submitted to the ordeal of formal portraiture.

"She looks like my daughter, Mister Shotton."

Shotton was nodding, furiously, trying to make a point.

"Lived hur. Thss hsss! Sssstr lived hur!"

"Good Lord. Did *you* then? When?"

"Nnn mmm, na, nnn mmm ssstr."

Shotton was struggling. He held up a finger and made a gesture of cutting it in half. Dad was lost. Shotton seized the pad and began to scribble. He drew the letter F then began what looked like a family tree, branching out from the F in two different directions. In one direction he wrote SISTER'S MOTHER, and, beneath it, MY SISTER. In the other he wrote MY MOTHER and, beneath it, ME.

"She was your half sister. Your father married twice?"

"Huf ssstr, ya. Huf ssstr. Mrd unce. Ony unce," and he drew a circle round MY MOTHER.

Dad held up the photograph and pointed to it. "Then

120

your sister ... your half sister ... was born outside marriage? She was, what did they call it, she was a love child?"

The old man nodded, slow and sad, and pointed to the door that led into the Coal House proper.

"Hur. Ya."

"When? When was all this?"

Shotton took the pad again. He began to write dates, pointing either at himself or at the girl's photograph to indicate the year of their births. By trying to follow and then writing down his own interpretation, Dad reached understanding. The girl had been born, in the Coal House, in 1887. She had died some time before Shotton was born. Shotton had been born in 1901 to the same father and a different mother.

"You never knew her, then."

"Nnn."

"How did you get the photograph?"

"Fthr. Mm fthr."

"So your father still saw his daughter, even after he married your mother?"

Shotton's right eye was moist. He shook his head.

"Nn. Nvr." He pointed into the Coal House and made a dismissive gesture. "Nnn l'low. Fthr nnn!" And he swept a final hand out and away from the house.

"Bloody hell," said Dad and jumped up. "Mister Shotton, I'm being an idiot. Wait here."

Within a few moments he was back, showing Shotton the press clipping of the little girl's death. The effect was puzzling. Shotton smoothed it out on the worktop and read it carefully. He read it again.

"Your half sister. Isn't it."

Shotton nodded and beckoned Dad to his side. As Dad watched, the old man's big index finger prodded the names of the dead girl: Martha, pause: Eleanor, pause: Patten.

When he pointed to the surname, Shotton nodded and tapped his head. When he pointed to the two Christian names, he shrugged and made a sign of ignorance.

"You mean, you never knew her name?"

Shotton seemed smaller. He looked at Dad and Dad saw the tears shine on the old man's good side. He also saw a movement of the twisted mouth. Shotton was trying to smile. Why? Shotton held up the clipping and pointed again:

". . .interment at Saint Lawrence Church."

The old man stood up and put his hat on. He pocketed the photograph and the press cutting. Dad wondered if Tommy Saddler's grandad would miss it, but couldn't bring himself to say anything. Shotton gripped his hand and shook it firmly. He was building up to the longest speech of that strange night.

"Thnk'y. Now. Ah. No. Whr ssstr. Uz."

He turned to the door and paused. On a window sill beside the door was Alison's school photograph, a uniform colour print in an oval card frame with a sheet of smaller contacts beside it. Dad hadn't got round to doing anything with them. Shotton looked down at them from his towering height.

"Yr dtr?"

"Yes. Alison."

Shotton patted the pocket that contained the portrait of his dead half-sister and looked at Dad. Dad nodded.

"Yes, they are, aren't they."

"G-nt. Thnk'y."

Dad followed the big man into the night. The wind had dropped a little, but not much. Leaves still whirled and trees creaked. Shotton turned, held up one arm in salute for a moment and paced off, through the stables and away towards the footpath that led to the lower village.

Of course. Until now, the Coal House had been his only connection with the dead girl. Until now. Shotton was on his way down to Saint Lawrence Church, in solitary search for a family he'd never known.

"Come again, Mister Shotton. Whenever you like."

Shotton paused and turned but did not speak or wave. The black cloak flapped and he was gone through the bushes into the night.

*

Dad heaved himself out of the telephone chair, took a deep breath and headed, haltingly, for the Leek Show. He limped up the drive, across the road and round the pub to the shed behind. It was not only unlocked, it was so filled with people there was a queue stretching out into the pub yard.

"The hell with that," grumbled Dad, hobbling away again. He couldn't face the stretch back to the Coal House without resting his ankle and used this as an excuse to potter into the pub. There, he saw Peter Robson leaning against the bar.

Peter was pie-eyed.

He was normally an abstemious man, but in the short half hour since the Leek Show Judges had emerged from the shed and pinned their findings on the pub board, Peter had swallowed his way to the outside of four pints of local, strong beer. He had not had to pay for one of them. When he saw Dad come through the door of the pub, Peter's day was complete.

"Morning, Peter. Like a . . ."

"Put your money away, Alec. This is mine."

Alec? Was this war or peace?

"I don't get it." Everyone was looking at Dad as if they shared a secret about him. By the smirks on their faces the secret was either very good or very embarrassing news. Geordie Harrison was wheezing happily in his corner. Ted Saddler was sucking happily at a pint, his eyes fixed on Dad through the eddying beer. Even dour Harry the landlord was smiling as he slid a pint towards Dad across a bartop littered with the debris of celebration. Peter Robson leaned forward, swayed, steadied himself and spoke into an almost complete silence.

"Ye came first, marrer! Y'bloody won an' all!"

There was a flowering of noise: shouted congratulations, laughs, whoops, toasts. Dad stood on one leg, nonplussed. For a second, he didn't understand. He had been thinking about Sue, Shotton, Alison. Now the world was shaking him by the hand and demanding that he remember other, more momentous matters.

"Not a year here and the bugger's won the Leeks!"

"Never live this one down, like."

"We'll have to give him a passport now."

"Mind, they were canny."

"You mean . . . our Leeks got First Prize?"

A chorus of "Why aye!" and "Of course, man!" and "What did y'think?"

"Good Lord."

"Y'hear that? He wins the Leeks and he says 'Good Lord'!"

"Well. I don't know what else to say."

"He doesn't know what else to say. Who'll tell him what the Leek Winner says?"

There was a hush. Peter Robson walked very carefully over to Dad and put a beery mouth to his ear. After a couple of false starts, he whispered the traditional formula into Dad's spinning brain.

"Oh," said Dad. "I see. Right then."

Dad banged his walking stick on the bar and utter silence fell. Harry the landlord flexed his fingers. All faces looked at Dad. Dad wished Alison were with him to see all this adulation. Anyway. Dad took a careful breath.

"Gentlemen. I'll fill the bar!"

Alison heard the cheers three quarters of a mile away as she toiled back up the farm path towards the Coal House. Celebrations in the pub. Leek Show? Probably. She saw an entire economy, a complete social structure revolving around those perfect, too-good-to-eat vegetables. Drinks were being bought, parties held, extravagances overlooked, all for the sake of vegetables and flowers.

Cheaper to buy them in the shops?

Yes. But less valuable.

The Coal House was empty except for a sleepy Cubby and a prowly Max. She felt aimless. She had a squirmy tummy and suspected she was about to start a period. If so, it would be early. Swimming on Monday, too. An aimless Saturday lunchtime. No Dad. Hang on, the car was in the

124

garage, so he couldn't be far away. She made a pickled onion sandwich and quartered the house. Max followed her as far as the ballroom, where the cat preferred to sit on the hearth, gazing at some embers left in the grate. Alison climbed upstairs and checked bathroom and bedrooms. Nobody. She peeked into Dad's bedroom. Snoozing? Nobody. She opened the windows and stepped out on the balcony.

Now that the leaves were off the trees she could see the bones of the landscape more clearly. Places usually hidden by foliage had crept nearer to the house, making it less isolated. A car climbed the hill towards the village. There was a movement in the trees which triggered some rooks and pigeons. They soared screeching and chattering up into a milky sky.

Alison leaned over the balcony and wondered what to do to waste the rest of the day. In the old orchard, a fox barked. A vixen. Dog foxes rarely barked. Tommy had said so.

The scene was monochrome except for the drifts of russet leaves. The fields were silvery grey with the autumn ploughing. That was it. She'd start stitching the rabbit skins together. A cloak for winter.

She was about to leave the balcony in search of needle and twine when something flapped and caught her eye.

It was pinned to the nearest sycamore, facing the balcony, a square of white which flashed and flickered in the weak sunlight.

She ran downstairs, waking Cubby, who stretched and scampered after her, looking for adventure. Outside, she trotted down the length of the house, round the corner, under the verandah and over to the tree.

She had to stand on tiptoe to reach it: a white envelope, wrapped in a wrinkled polythene bag and tacked to the bark. She sat on the grass, her back to the tree and opened the bag. On the envelope, in bright blue ink was the one word ALISON, written in careful capital letters that sloped slightly from left to right in the way that children write when they hold their heads too close to the paper, squinting

125

sideways with concentration.

She thought of Tommy Saddler. Hardly. Anyway, he couldn't write that neatly, his schoolwork was a disaster.

The envelope was tubby with its contents. She opened it and took out the photograph of Martha Eleanor Patten. She knew who it was immediately, without having any reason to know who it was. Tucked inside the card folder was a sheet of thick, old paper, covered with sloping, bright blue writing. She opened it out and started to read.

"*Dear Alison . . .*"

"Hi. What on earth are you up to?"

Sue. She stood by the verandah post, posing prettily. She wore a fur jacket and pink ski pants. Oh hell.

"Where's your Dad?"

"Dunno, really."

"Only we had a mini-fight on the telling-bone. Thought I'd come and sweeten things up."

"It's Leek Show day. Maybe he's over there."

"Yes, he said. Oh well, I suppose I'd better go and investigate. Coming?"

Alison caved in. She wanted to read the unexpected letter, but Sue made it awkward. She'd keep it for later.

"Homework," she said, stuffing the letter in her pocket. "Come on then, let's go and find the old sod."

"Alison!"

Goody. She'd shocked the unshockable Sue.

They found him sprawled in a chair in the pub, in the middle of a group of equally sprawled regulars and Leek Club devotees.

"I've won," he said, and hiccoughed.

They manhandled Dad down the drive to the Coal House. He complained about his ankle a great deal, but with volume and no intimation of pain. Together, they stretched him on the sofa. He giggled.

Sue considered him and turned to Alison.

"Look, can you make some black coffee?"

"He doesn't like black coffee."

"That's not the point, dear. Make some. Then I'll put

126

him to bed."

Alison had been turning in the direction of the kitchen. She stopped abruptly. She turned to face Sue and said:

"I beg your pardon?"

"I'll put him to bed. Sleep it off. Best thing."

"You? Put my Dad to bed?" She remembered a picked-up phrase of Maisie's. "Sister, you've lost your thread."

Sue stared at her and slowly smiled.

"Well, well. Hello Alison."

"Hello yourself. You make the coffee. I'll put him to bed. My way."

The two women stared at each other. The two cats tore through the open kitchen door, through the living room and upstairs, chasing, playing and snapping the moment in two.

"All right, Alison."

"Good."

She fetched a spare blanket and tucked Dad up. He grinned and opened his eyes. Blearily, they found her as she leaned over him.

"H'llo."

"Hello yourself. You're drunk, you disgusting old man."

"True, very true."

"But you never get drunk. Well, not so's I'd notice."

"Leeks."

"You know where the bog is."

"Ho ho. Won the Leeks. Big thing. Up here. Never heard of. Not before. Big thing. Sorry, Ally."

"That's OK. Well done, I suppose, though I think it was more Peter than you, mind."

Dad smiled like a cherub, then frowned and said:

"Who's that destroying the kitchen?"

It was Alison's turn to smile. She fetched the coffee, made sure that Dad was asleep and snoring with his mouth open, left the coffee to grow cold and went upstairs to read her letter.

Sue went home.

Chapter 10

On the day after her daughter's funeral, Elizabeth Patten revisited the grave, without telling anyone.

George was at the Pit Office, sternly soldiering as if nothing had happened. Indeed, the moment the funeral service had finished, the very minute they all walked from the graveside, life had resumed for everyone around her. It was as if Nellie had never been. She hated the Northern stoicism, the brief, grudging admittance of sorrow and the swift return to the business of the living. She hated the North. Southern born and raised, she had struggled against the match with George Patten and not because she necessarily disliked the man. He was kind in a gruff way, solid and substantial. She also understood that the nation's wealth sprang from the earth of the North and she should not deny its place in her life. She simply hated the bleak, drear dirt that accompanied the gaining of that wealth.

Nellie had helped. Nellie could help no longer. She was lying deep in that same bleak, drear dirt. She was a part of Elizabeth that was decaying in the earth which lay above the coal George mined, hundreds of feet beneath her daughter's coffin. Coal. She hated coal.

It was a chill autumn morning, with frost still shining beside the hedges as she walked from the house, down the footpath towards the farm and the church of Saint Lawrence. To her right, a pitheap loomed and smoked, waggons squealed, men bellowed. The winding gear shrieked in the cold air as the mid-morning shift changed and soiled bodies were hauled from the darkness to stumble, blinking, into daylight, while others, starched in linen and creaking in leather, took their places and were dropped like dross to the depths.

There was a stutter of coal trucks on the pit line, an engine huffed, a bell clanged and a siren howled. A gust of dusty, meaty smell raced through the hawthorn hedge and across her face. From the day she'd arrived in the coalfield, she'd been aware of the reek of coal smoke. It was familiar to her from her home in the South, but here it was rawer, more pervasive. Her clothes carried clinging smuts, her hair grew lank, her lungs complained and still George defended the war he waged on the countryside. There were no flowers left, no clear streams, the very sycamore trees coughed and survived. Birds fluttered into the coalfield, pecked and flew away, heading for the far moors beyond the city. Even George's hunters stood in the paddock with hung heads, looking different from their sisters, the pitponies, only in that their eyes were slightly clearer, their coats more carefully groomed. Their spirit was no different. The local hunt had caught no fox for three years. The very animals had withdrawn in horror and despair.

She crossed the plank bridge over the beck, skirted the farmhouse and started the gentle slope up towards the graveyard. Yesterday, they had entered from the front, carriages ranked on the gravel, black plumes bending in a soft breeze, voices low, elbows held, vicar and rector bowing them into the church. The organ had coughed, wheezed and whispered sympathetic tunes. The coffin had been carried by six of George's men. Later, the air was smoky between the avenues of gravestones. Harrison and Saddler were standing with shovels and wearing leather aprons, hats in their hands.

"Dust to dust . . ."

George had thrown his clod of earth downwards, turned away and steered her towards home. She had heard Harrison and Saddler begin to shovel in the soil with the measured economy of the lifelong pitmen they were. George would pay them three shillings each for the morning's special duties. Six shillings to cover Nellie with dark, gritty, coal-rich earth.

The church was partly hidden behind bare trees. She ignored it and turned right, her steps quickening to the grave.

They had pressed turves of yellowing grass over the freshly dug earth, and the squares did not yet join or marry. It was a ramshackle, makeshift effect. On the fresh, new stone she noticed that the stonemason had chipped the 'a' of Eleanor. George had chosen the inscription from a book provided by the undertaker: it was banal and could be seen on any of a score of headstones in the graveyard. She ignored the inscription as she ignored the church and concentrated only on the ring of flowers she had asked to be laid on top of the grave.

Kneeling on the ground, she gently touched the flowers and saw black coal smuts already lodged in the blossoms. Even the flowers looked weary. If a flower could wheeze, these would.

"Oh Nell. Dear Nell. Don't go?"

Silence. Of course. She was being silly. But.

"You've left me alone, Nell."

"Aye, and more than you, Elizabeth."

She did not need to turn round to know who was casting a pale shadow over the grave. She took her time, watching the way the long cloak stretched its shade across the length of Nellie's plot, how the wide-brimmed hat was echoed on the headstone. Slowly, she stood and turned to face him.

"Ernest."

"Elizabeth."

"Why are you here?" she asked, then blushed with the stupidity of the question. The big man looked down at her and twisted out a wry smile.

"I was not invited to the funeral, Elizabeth. I must visit when I may, then. I am your husband's Pit Foreman, I can come and go a little. I came to read the lie carved on that

130

headstone."

"Only you and I know it is a lie, Ernest."

"One day I shall put it to rights. 'Martha Eleanor, Beloved Daughter of . . . Ernest Shotton and Elizabeth Patten.' The truth, eh, lass?"

"Ernest, you wouldn't! You must never . . ."

"Hush up. We've kept the secret thirteen years. Why would I break it now? Why, your husband would have my job and you would be banished. What good can we do our daughter now?"

"We have no daughter now."

"You don't believe that."

"No. I don't believe that."

She was not sure about letting him hold her but when he did, she was glad. She drained into his powerful arms. His black cloak was rough and comforting.

"Do you know, lass," he said, his voice rumbling against her cheek, "I reckon this is the first time we've said more than 'Good Day' for all of those thirteen years?"

"I was very young. Very lonely. George has never been an easy man. When he thought, when he believed he was to be a father, I thought, I just prayed it would soften him. Though I knew how much it would hurt you."

"Hush up. What could I give Nellie? A Pit Foreman's cottage? Old women to tend her? She lived in the Colliery Manager's house and wanted for nowt. I watched her grow. I saw her, now and then. There's a heap of trouble in this world without shouting that the Manager's a cuckold by his own Foreman."

She pulled back and looked under the brim of his hat at the clear, grey eyes.

"Was it you, then? Walking? Do you?"

He gazed at her for several moments, then nodded.

"I walk by your house when I can, Elizabeth. Usually at night, but in daylight if my shift says so. I like to look at the place where you and my daughter live. Lived. I do no harm. Just look and imagine."

"Nell saw you, several times, I think. She did not know

131

who you were. She died not knowing who you were, Ernest."

"I think I saw her die. I saw her fall. I wanted to come to the house. I could not."

"We found her by the window, by the balcony."

"Aye, lass, that would be it."

"What will you do?"

"I will marry and live on. What will you do?"

"Marry? Whom?"

"I said, what will you do?"

"Why . . . carry on, I suppose."

"You see, Elizabeth? I walk the woods and think of my daughter. You will 'carry on'. I shall marry and save what I can from life. A lass from the village. She has waited ower long. She will do."

She wanted to strike him. "So you have left me too!"

His face changed so gradually she could not say when it became bitter.

"Elizabeth. For thirteen years I have behaved to you as your husband's Foreman, not the father of your child. I agreed to that. While Nellie lived, I lived. For thirteen years you have given me nothing but Nellie. Now that she's gone, you can take no more from me. Haway, lass, it is time I pretended to be alive. And I promise you this . . ."

He gripped her arms so hard that she shrank and squirmed.

". . . I shall bring my children to the woods and I shall tell them: There, that's where your half-sister lived. That is where you can be. Work. Think. The people who live in that big house are no better than you. They behave no better. That could be yours. You could be there."

He thrust her away, regarded her, turned and paced off towards the church gate. He heard her running after him but continued to walk. She reached him at the gate and tugged at his cloak.

"Ernest. I should like you to have this. I have one, too."

She was fumbling in her bag while he waited, immensely tall, profoundly black. When she handed him the rectangle of cardboard he looked briefly, painfully, at the photograph of his daughter before putting it away in an inside pocket. He touched the brim of his hat.

"Mistress Patten."

"Mister Shotton."

"God help us both, Elizabeth."

"Amen, Ernest."

He was gone, stalking back to the Colliery and the duties he knew so well. He was walking into a future that held the sorrow of a son who would scream beneath the earth.

Through her tears, Elizabeth Patten watched him take her life with him.

*

Dear Alison,

Am writing you this note because I would like you to have this photograph of my sister Martha Eleanor who we your Dad and I think looks just like you. I do not need it now because your Dad helped me find where she is. Would like you to have it because you look the same and you live in the Coal House just like Martha Eleanor. Your Dad was kind to me and asked me to come back but I wont because I know I frighten people and it would not be fair. I hope you are happy and I hope you live a long and happy life in the Coal House. It is a pity you do not have a brother or a sister I think it must be good to have one. Perhaps you will have lots of children of your own one day a happy family is a strong thing. Kind regards.

Arthur Shotton

Alison put the photograph on the windowsill of her bedroom, where she could see it from her pillow. She thought about the letter for a long time. Her first reaction had been to find Dad and ask him who Arthur Shotton was and where Martha Eleanor was and how Dad had found her. She stopped herself. There was too much going on. She thought of the Leek Show, the village, the books and bills, Peter, Sue's expectant friendship, she saw Dad asleep with beer and escape and she saw that he had made a

133

friendship beyond all that. It was Dad's secret. Arthur
Shotton had let her into it, but Dad didn't know that. If he
wanted to tell her, he would. She would keep the secret
until he felt like sharing it.

She felt rewardingly noble.

She went to find the needle and twine. She would hide her
secret under a furry cloak.

Christmas hung on the horizon. Messages came from the
South: Gran was ill, she and Grandpa couldn't come. Not,
thought Alec, that he'd got round to suggesting it.

"It's a rotten shame, Dad. All this room . . ."

"Maybe in the summer . . ."

The year's weather patterns stayed erratic. Cold air
washed down from the Arctic, hammering temperatures
deep into the ground and proving the milkman's moles right,
the postmistress's birds wrong.

"What about your old buddy, Sal? Would she like to come
up during the hols?"

"She's gone to Lanzarotte with her Mum and Dad."

"But I thought . . ."

"Not her real Dad. He's going to be her new one."

"That was quick."

"Doesn't take some people long."

Clouds of snow iced the landscape. Fog fell, rose, fell
again. Cars crunched on the motorway. Black ice was
forecast and duly arrived.

"When I was your age, ice didn't have a colour. It was just
ice."

"Modern ice has to be black or it doesn't count. Ice is
ethnic."

"Ally, stop it. You're growing up to be sophisticated.
That'll never do."

She followed her new policy of not putting Dad under any
extra pressure. She saved her pocket money, caught a bus
into the city one Saturday morning and bought a generous
length of lining fabric, a rich, churchy crimson. She'd

134

settled on Dad's Christmas present. She'd told Tommy Saddler, prodding him into a higher rate of rabbit skin production.

"It's not long now. I haven't got nearly enough yet."

"Bugger that, bonny lass, you canna bag bunnies if there's nae bunnies t'bag! They're all hibernating, like."

"Rabbits don't hibernate."

"How'd you know, then?"

"I saw their footprints in the snow this morning. Get out there and get on with it. Bonny lad."

Every day, Alison went out on the balcony and checked the nearest sycamore. There were no more letters. She itched to ask Dad, but didn't. She looked up the name Shotton in the local telephone directory. There was a page and a half of them. She asked Billy the milkman. He delivered to twenty-seven Shottons in a radius of ten miles. She gave up.

Sue was taking Christmas seriously.

There was a campaign afoot to prise Dad and Alison away from the Coal House and into a cosy, hi-fi stereo and telly Christmas in the city.

"We could go to the Carol Concert in the Cathedral, all three of us."

"It's not a Concert, it's a Service."

"Yes. Well. Same thing."

"No, it isn't, actually."

Alison foresaw the problems if Sue got them for Christmas. It would be like a bad, old, Hollywood movie. Dad would be Bing Crosby, Sue would be June Allyson, she would be the token-child. They'd open presents round the tree, carve the turkey together, crack nuts and pull crackers. Even the colours of caring would be as washed-out as an old piece of celluloid film. But the Marriage Certificate would be as good as signed, in sentiment, if not in fact.

Sue was clearly out for a final conclusion. Alison was undecided. Should her new don't-worry-Dad policy go so far as to let Sue have her way? She bided her time and thought hard.

The school term dribbled to an end in a welter of plays, trips and reports. Maisie and Alison vied for top form position and shared it. Edith was sniffy, but not for long. Alone of the three, Edith had a boyfriend, a skinny, ginger stick who took her to the pictures and bought her chips.

"His Dad's a farmer, too."

"Well, that's it, then."

"What?"

"They probably talk about unshorn heavy hoggets."

"What are they?"

"Don't know. Farmy things."

On the day school broke up, a week before Christmas, the snow came.

It poured from gunmetal skies for three days and four nights. The Northeast wind was there, but slack, so the snow did not drift. It simply piled itself silently, deeper and deeper, painting the trees and plastering the walls. Cubby and Max, new to snow, took to disappearing into it in vain search of vanished mice. For her first winter, Alison felt no need to build a snowman or throw snowballs, though she had never been presented with so much raw material. Instead, she wrapped up, rummaged for her wellies and plodged round the garden and over to the village, enjoying the flawless purity and watching how the snow replaced familiar landscapes with stark engravings, in which dark shapes sprang out of their backgrounds and took on extra meaning.

Geordie Harrison and Harry the landlord, alone in the pub, stood by the blazing fire and watched Alison from the bar window.

"White Christmas, then, Geordie?"

"Looks like it. By, I canna remember when we had this much this early, mind."

Dad tried to get the car up the drive and failed. The snow plough had been through the village, banking snow right across the entrance to the Coal House. They were sealed in. Dad hiked to the lower village and filled a rucksack with essential provisions. He hiked back, panting, and rewarded himself with a hot pie and a pint in the pub.

"Saw your lass out in the snow this morning. Enjoying it, is she?"

"Think so, Geordie. She's pretty offhand about things these days. Much more interested that her anorak matches her eyes and her gloves match her scarf."

"Aye, that's the way of it, like. Your lady friend coming out for Christmas, is she?"

Sue always made a point of buying Geordie a brown ale, which had lodged her in the old boy's mind more firmly than any red hair, long legs or white boiler suits could have done.

"Couldn't say, Geordie. Might not be able to get."

Dad munched his pie and tried to decide whether or not he wanted to spend Christmas with Sue in the city. He decided he didn't. Did he want Sue to spend Christmas at the Coal House? He decided he was undecided. The previous Christmas had been messy. He and Alison had stayed with Gran and Grandpa, silent in the aftermath of Helen's death. He wanted this Christmas to make up for all that. And he no longer ached for adult company: Alison was company enough, he was pleased to admit to himself. Even so, scissors disappeared. Scraps of red cloth were to be found attached to chairs and carpets. She spent long hours in her room. He was apprehensive. The Saddler boy had been seen in the woods with his rifle. Dad was suspicious.

He went home. Almost immediately, the phone rang. Sue.

"Well?"

"What?"

"Christmas. Well?"

"Here. Definitely. Please come. Stay, Sue, do."

Sue sat in her flat in the city, looking out at the Cathedral. She held the telephone away from her ear. It wasn't going to work, was it? Was it? No. Oh well, let's have Christmas, at least.

"Alec, I'd love to. What should I bring?"

Later, when she put the phone down, she had a picture of the girl in her mind. Alison. How had she done it? Done it, she somehow had. Did it matter? Probably not. She would be a clever woman, no doubt. Sisters under the skin. But, my, she'd started early.

Sue sniffed and went in search of tissues.

Dad looked like a rabbit. He actually looked like a rabbit.

He stood in front of the mirror in the living room, the cloak draped over his shoulders and he stuck his two front teeth out, under his top lip. Then he twitched his nose. It was uncanny.

"Dad, why do you look like a rabbit?"

"Because I'm covered in rabbit skins. And anyway, I'm being hunted from pillar to post."

"By whom, may I ask?"

"Bank Manager. Agent. Publisher. Sue."

"Me?"

"Oh no, thank God, not you."

"Then why thank God?"

"Sorry, thank you."

"Hold still a mo."

She had decided to come clean and tell Dad what he was getting for Christmas. She couldn't fit the thing right without a session with pins and mirrors. Dad had been childishly pleased, though what he'd do with a rabbit skin cloak defeated her. He was in a funny mood, wasting the days until Christmas with work, worry and an air of what-the-hell. Alison quite liked it. She was still waiting to hear about Mister Arthur Shotton and Martha Eleanor, but there were no indications that Dad was ready to spill the beans.

"Sue's coming for Christmas."

"Triffic."

"Well. Why not?"

"Why not indeed. As long as she does her share of the washing-up."

It stopped snowing. The night before Christmas Eve, Alison couldn't sleep and lay in bed gazing out of the window at the silver snowscape of the garden. Martha's

138

picture got in the way and she moved it, feeling the crackle of the letter she had paper-clipped to the back of the folder. An owl called in the trees. It was almost midnight.

She saw the black figure while it was still a long way from the house, walking steadily through the stark trees, lifting its feet high to cope with the snow. It seemed to flicker, black on white, as it passed behind the tree trunks.

She knew who it was she was watching. When the figure turned from the old drive and headed for the nearest sycamore, she was certain. She hadn't much time. A pullover, some socks, a dressing gown and, as she raced through the kitchen, a quick shrug into her wellies. The night air was silky but not cold. Cubby was sitting on the courtyard wall and staring at Alison with night-fighting eyes that shone with moonlight. Alison swept past and down the side of the house, blessing the silent snow. She paused at the corner, peering round and through the verandah pillars.

It was standing by the sycamore, carefully tacking another white envelope to the bark. It half turned, to check that the envelope was visible from the balcony above. Alison stepped forward and the tall black figure froze, its head turned towards her, its face in shadow.

"Good evening, Mister Shotton."

The owl called in the woods again. They both glanced into the trees. Alison looked back first and saw the moonlight full on Arthur Shotton's face. So that was it. Her finger nails bit into her palms and she knew that she must not be silly now.

"You wrote me that nice letter. Thanks. And thanks for Martha's photograph. I keep it in my bedroom."

"Ysss." Arthur looked at her, keeping the brim of his hat low.

"You mustn't worry about frightening me, Arthur." She took a deep breath and told a lie. "Dad told me all about your face, it's all right."

She stepped forward and up to the sycamore, where the ground swelled round the trunk, putting Alison on the same level as the huge old man. She reached forward, gently, and took the black hat from Shotton's head. She looked at him and smiled.

"See? It's all right." Shotton's good eye widened and blinked. Alison said: "You look a bit like an owl that's given itself a fright, that's all."

"Mmth." A noise of incredulity, gratitude.

"Is it a Christmas Card?"

"Ysss. Hrrr."

Shotton reached up and unpinned the envelope. When he handed it to her she saw the familiar blue printed letters: ALISON & HER FATHER.

She opened the envelope and withdrew a rectangle of stiff, white card. On it was a drawing of the Coal House, seen through the trees from the old driveway. It was a fine sketch, done with black felt tip pen and soft pencil. Entwined in the undergrowth at the bottom of the picture were the two, tiny letters, *A.S.* On the reverse of the card, the sloping blue writing again: *Happy Christmas. A. Shotton.*

"It's super. Thank you." And she leaned forward and kissed his cheek. He was trembling with fear.

"Fancy a cuppa tea?"

"Uh. Ysss. Thnk'y, vrrr mch."

"Come on then. We've got masses to talk about."

She took the old man's hand and led him through the moonlit snow towards the kitchen.

On Christmas Eve morning, Sue crawled out of her bed in the flat and wavered into the bathroom. Her tongue was covered with creamy fur. Her temperature was high. Her forehead burned. She coughed and her head pulsed. She felt as if she stood inside a transparent box. She smiled a rueful snarl at the mirror, then smiled properly but unhappily.

"Not only do I lose, I get kicked when I'm down."

At the end of the telephone, Alec said "You've got what?"

" 'Flu, my dear. Influenza. I feel like a corpse."

"But you can't have! You're coming here for Christmas!"

140

"No, Alec. I'm going to bed. I'd be no company and I'd probably pass it on." She coughed. "Hear me? I sound like a fox. No, Christmas, for me, is cancelled. I'll bring your pressies over when I'm human again." Click.

He went in search of his daughter and found her by the greenhouse, with Tommy Saddler. Between them, a dead rabbit lay in the snow.

She was saying "You might have managed two or three more. That's all I needed. It takes a week to cure them."

"Aw, Alison, man, it's Christmas Eve!"

Alison sounded perversely sulky: "Didn't know rabbits celebrated Christmas. You could've tried a bit harder, a bit earlier."

Tommy appealed to the skies. "I canna conjure them out of nowt, now canna?"

"Quite right, Tommy. Never let a woman get the habit of making unreasonable demands."

"But, Dad . . ."

"Shush. I don't mind if my cloak's not finished until after Christmas. Anyway, they'd go stiff: Peter couldn't get new ones cured before January."

"*Your* cloak, like?" gawped Tommy. "I thought *she* . . ."

"No. I am to be Rabbit King of the Coal House. I shall wear it for inspiration when I'm working."

"Why, bugger."

"Tommy, you've done wondrously already. Come with me."

Dad led them to the kitchen, whistling and swinging the rabbit, which he dumped on the draining board before continuing through the house to the ballroom, where a log fire struggled and the Christmas tree stood self-consciously in a corner. Dad rummaged among the presents at its foot and sang a carol. Tommy nudged Alison and raised an eyebrow. Alison shrugged. Her Dad was high on something and therefore dangerously unpredictable. Dad straightened and handed Tommy a heavy, sausage-shaped packet.

"Merry Christmas, faithful bunny-murderer."

It was a Swiss Army pocket knife with all the gadgets.

141

"Ee, the bugger!"

"Tommy, have you ever thought of stretching your vocabulary? You know, just a few new words, now and again, just for variety's sake?"

"Ee, thanks Mister Lucas, it's great, like."

"Glad you like it. Now. I fancy a glass of dry sherry. Care to join me?"

He turned towards the living room, then paused and turned to Alison.

"Oh, by the way, Sue just rang. She's ill. Poorly. Can't make it over."

"Oh. Dearie me."

"Yes. Bit sad, really. Come on."

Some more snow fell on Christmas night, a light, swirling fall that served to smooth out the footmarks and paw prints that criss-crossed the courtyard of the Coal House. Over at the pub, lights blazed and Harry perspired as he rushed from order to order. Seasonal music was playing on a looped tape cassette: he'd heard "Jingle Bells" seven times that evening already.

"Bottle o' broon ale, bonny lad, please."

"Aye, right you are, Geordie."

Dad and Alison walked out into the snow and began an aimless circuit of the house. Dad puffed a Christmas cigar. Their feet creaked in the thick white night. They paused by the stables and looked across to the blazing pub and the village, its windows studded with Christmas lights.

"Do you want to pop over for a pint?"

"No. I'd rather stay here. We'll build the fire up. Phone Gran later. It's peaceful here. Probably too peaceful for you?"

"No. S'OK."

They walked on, round to the lawn, out on to the stretch of white. Two ginger, black and white missiles scorched past them, spraying snow as they chased and jumped.

"Sorry the cloak isn't ready."

142

"Like I said, doesn't matter a bit."

They paused by the trees and looked back at the Coal House, clear against the snow and the black sky. Dad had been putting this moment off for a long time, fearing what it might bring. Tonight, in the cool air, he had the feeling that he need not have worried so much. He took a deep breath.

"Ally?"

"What?"

"How would you like to move to the city? Buy a proper house? There's a chance I can do some supplementary lecturing at the university, help things along a bit. You could go to the City School, it's very good. Then, later, maybe, the university, though you could take a flat or stay in a hall of residence, you wouldn't have to live at home, I always thought having a place of your own was half the fun of being an undergraduate. There wouldn't be so much garden, so I'd do more work in the study and there'd be more for you to do without having to trek around in buses. Meet more people."

"I suppose Sue's part of this fairy tale existence?"

Dad blew a perfect smoke ring at the stars which were appearing above the Coal House.

"I suppose she would be, really. I suppose."

"She'd never come and live here, would she?"

"Um. No, she wouldn't. She's made that plain."

"That's a pity, really. You see, I can't leave the Coal House."

"No. Neither can I, really."

"You see, Dad, I have to be here as long as the owl needs me to be here."

Dad took his cigar out of his mouth and looked at her curiously. "Owl?"

"Arthur Shotton. Martha's brother."

"How on earth . . ."

"Aha. He sent us a Christmas card, you know. I was saving it for the morning. Smashing picture of the house."

"Well, I'll be . . ."

"You really ought to stretch your vocabulary. And anyway,

there's another reason we're not shifting."

"Go on."

"Mum might not know where to find us."

"She'll always find us. When we need her. When she needs us."

"And there's another reason."

"What?"

"Tommy Saddler owes us at least two more rabbit skins."

Dad laughed. "Very true. So we stay."

"Don't be daft. 'Course we do."

He smiled at his daughter and caught her hand.

"OK. We stay. Now, about that school ski-trip . . ."

Alison Lucas held hands with her tatty Dad and walked, talking, back through the snow towards the Coal House.